TWO BLOSSOMS ON A SINGLE STEM

By **GWENETH HOWARD MAHONEY**

Illustrated by **ELIZABETH HOWARD CARNES**

DEDICATION

This is for my family: those who came before me and those who carry on ahead

ISBN-13: 978-1514140451

ISBN-10: 1514140454

Contents

Part One: This Is My Father's World

Corbally, County Tyrone, Ireland
Summer 1909

Chapter 1
All Nature Sings

A rough hand clamped around Winnie's throat, draining the air from her lungs. A scream lodged itself deep inside her aching throat. She was falling through a dark earthen tunnel with no bottom.

Eleven-year-old Winnie Weir awoke with a jerk. Another nightmare!

Still shaking, drenched in perspiration despite the early morning chill, Winnie pulled away a scratchy blanket from her neck. Across the small farmhouse, Winnie could hear wee Tommy stirring on his mattress beside Ma and Da's bed. From the corner of the bed she shared with her two sisters, she scanned the room.

Beside her, fourteen-year-old Annie breathed evenly, sound asleep. Sixteen-year-old Emily was already out of bed, standing before a dingy mirror, splashing water from a basin onto her face.

Winnie burrowed deeper into the warmth of her bed. She'd been plagued by these nightmares ever since her family had suffered through the terrible scarlet fever. Now, three years later, Winnie could not forget it.

Previously, the family had lived in Clabby, County Tyrone, in cramped quarters behind Da's shop. One by one, the fever had attacked each family member. All but William had survived.

Poor William, just five years old. Winnie remembered the pain on Da's face when he'd found William dead in his little cot. Cradling William's limp body in his arms, the lines on Da's face deepened and his body quaked. Winnie had never seen a grown-up cry before.

And she remembered how Ma's face had shut tight like a cupboard. Ever since William's death, Ma had gone inside herself. Before the scarlet fever, Ma had been a stately woman with regal carriage, proud of her British Protestant heritage. But now she was a shadow of a person. She had locked out everyone except Da and Emily. Da said this was Ma's way of grieving and that she'd get better.

He had moved the family a few miles away from the shop into this old farmhouse in Corbally, abandoned when a farmer's widow had died. The new life on a farm was supposed to cure Ma of her sadness, but Winnie wondered. Ma had given birth to Tommy two and a half years ago and was expecting another baby this winter. All she could do was drag herself out of bed to sip a little tea and nibble some toast. Then she went back to bed. Emily, Annie, and Winnie were left to tend wee Tommy and the house, while Da worked in the pasture.

Emily looked over and said, "Come along, Winnie. Annie, time to get up!"

"I'm coming," Winnie said, reluctantly kicking off the blankets. She scurried to the closet and pulled on an old dress and stockings. Glancing at Emily, she admired her oldest sister's long honey-colored braids and lace at the collar of her dress. She looked just like a fairy tale princess. Winnie's eyes dropped down to her hand-me-down shift. She looked like a scullery maid.

"Annie, you've got to get up," said Emily. "You need to start the fire."

Leaving Emily to coax sleepy Annie from bed, Winnie dashed out the scullery door, bucket in hand. Breathing in the sweet damp summer air, she ran to the well the family shared with several neighbors. The dewy grass tickled her bare feet. She was too impatient to put on her worn black leather shoes, hand-me-downs from her sisters. Besides, wearing them was nearly the same as having bare feet, the leather was so worn, especially just below each big toe. Her sisters had inherited bunions, an affliction that plagued the Weir family, and all of their shoes had a worn circle on its side. Winnie herself was starting to show signs of a bunion, and her foot fell into the worn pattern of the leather quite naturally.

After drawing water from the well, Winnie walked back to the house, trying her best not to splash. This fresh water would be used to make the tea and boil the eggs. Water for washing was collected in barrels beneath the overhanging tin roof.

Next, Winnie dashed to the hen house, her favorite chore.

"Clucky, Clucky, tch, tch, tch," Winnie called. The hens were locked in the hen house for the night, safe from foxes. As Winnie unlatched the rickety door, the hens circled and squawked in anticipation of the grain she would pitch to them.

"What have you got for us today, Clucky?" Winnie asked the oldest hen. "Ah, I spy a lovely brown egg for my breakfast! And how about the rest of you? Have you got something for Da and Ma as well?" Winnie hummed a tune as she collected a basket of eggs. She was disappointed to find only five eggs today. That meant that there'd be less than one egg for each family member.

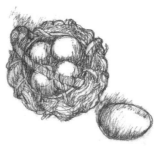

She reminded herself to tell Emily how many eggs were laid today, since Emily was so good with numbers. Emily had a special talent for calculating figures, and she enjoyed finding out how productive the hens were. Winnie preferred words, reading, and most of all, a good tale told by Da.

Through the back door, Winnie delivered the eggs to the scullery, where Annie was slicing bread.

"Morning, Winnie. Looks like you were in a mighty hurry to start your chores. Where are your shoes?" Annie scowled down at her. A full head taller than Winnie, she had the look of a young colt. She had not quite grown into her long legs, but she knew how to use her height to her advantage when it came to scolding Winnie.

"Annie, it's summertime. No need to be so proper. It's not as if we have to dress for school." Winnie shrugged. She was used to Annie's admonishments.

"Go on, then, Winnie, get yourself dressed for breakfast. I'll put the eggs in the pot to boil." Annie looked into the basket Winnie had delivered and frowned. "Only five eggs today? That's not enough."

Winnie set her hands on her hips. "You'll need to bring your complaints to Clucky, not me." She was in motion once again, scurrying through the front room of the house. Winnie could run from end to end of her family's rectangular cottage in a blink. Still, even with a scullery the size of a closet and two small bedrooms on either end of a main room, this house seemed a palace compared to her last home. Living here in Corbally was a step ahead, Da had said, but sometimes Winnie wondered how far they'd actually stepped. Da worked so hard from dawn 'til dusk, yet meals seemed as scant as ever.

On her way through the house, Winnie glimpsed Ma moving

with great effort to sit at the table. Winnie paused. Maybe today Ma would feel better. "Good morning, Ma."

A flicker of acknowledgment passed through Ma's face as she rested her hands on the top of her belly and said in a hoarse voice, "Morning." Winnie dipped down to kiss the side of Ma's cheek. How she longed for Ma to kiss her back.

Stepping in from the scullery, Annie said, "Still haven't fetched your shoes? And before you leave the room, put some more peat on the fire."

Winnie sighed. Had Annie meant to interrupt her quiet moment with Ma?

She headed to the hearth to tend the fire. Hanging from an iron hook above the flames, a black kettle dangled over the fire, the water within just beginning to steam.

On the floor before the hearth sat little Tommy. At two years old, he was always into mischief, and someone, probably Emily, had set out a spoon and several wooden bowls for his entertainment. Winnie paused to watch him stack the bowls, and without waiting to admire his tower, swing his spoon with great gusto, knocking the stack down. He clapped his dimpled hands and looked up at Winnie for approval.

"Oh, Tommy, what would we do without your racket?" Winnie patted his silken hair and proceeded to her room.

The girls' bedroom was sparsely furnished with a wooden bureau and a cast iron bed. Winnie snatched her everyday shoes from the closet and stuffed her feet into them hastily. A cardboard box caught her eye. Bending down, Winnie opened the box to inhale the rich smell of new leather. Her Sunday shoes were carefully polished, wrapped in tissue paper, and stowed away in pristine condition until next Sunday. Da said that his wealthy American sister had been so kind to send these shoes to them and the girls should be deeply grateful. Sometimes it was hard for Winnie to feel deeply grateful when the stiff leather pinched her bunion, especially during a long Sunday sermon.

Next, she stood up and gave herself a brief assessment in the small mirror, frowning at her over-sized front teeth. Her thick brown hair had escaped from the braids she'd plaited yesterday. Not one to dwell on appearances, Winnie reached for a book of poems upon the bureau and started to read.

"Breakfast is ready!" Annie called.

Using a hair ribbon as a book mark, Winnie closed her book. She rushed to the wooden table the family used for every meal. Sitting across from Da, who had just come in from milking the cows, the girls squeezed together on a bench. Little Tommy sat high on a chair Da had built when Emily was a toddler.

"Let us pray," Da said, and the family pressed their hands together. Once the prayer was over, everyone but Ma plunged their spoons into soft-boiled eggs.

"Please pass the toast and jam, Emily," asked Winnie.

"Do you mean, 'May I please have some toast beneath my strawberry jam?'" teased Emily. Da and Annie joined in good-natured laughter, as Winnie blushed in embarrassment. It was true that she adored strawberries.

Tommy spent most of the meal banging his spoon against the table, but somehow managed to consume a tin cup of milk, half an egg, and a bit of toast.

Ma hadn't finished the other half of his egg, and as usual, she didn't seem to have much of an appetite. Winnie thought it odd that pregnancy made Ma sick to her stomach. How would the baby inside her grow if Ma didn't eat?

They washed down their breakfasts with strong Irish tea, which was a little too bitter for Winnie's taste as there were only a few grains of sugar stuck in the bottom of the sugar bowl. No matter, the girls were eager to begin their day.

"It's off to the fields for me. One of the cows has taken sick. Needs some tending." Da stood up and smoothed his wavy brown hair. He adjusted his worn jacket across his broad shoulders. Winnie noticed that his sideburns and mustache were sprinkled with a few gray hairs. Since when did Da look so old? Da seemed to feel Winnie's eyes upon him, and he winked, his mouth breaking into a contagious big toothed grin. "Be sure to tidy up for Ma, girls." He stood behind Ma's chair and wrapped his arms around her from the back, his large hands gently patting Ma's belly. "Make sure you get some rest for that new baby, Isabella." Ma angled her head towards him, a faint smile on her face. Da reached for his tweed cap hanging from a nail in the wall and left the house, heading for the tumble-down barn.

"Let me wash up." Winnie claimed her preferred chore.

"All right . . . I'll dry the ware if you wash, but please don't spend so much time playing with the water," said Annie.

Winnie sighed. She knew she had a bad habit of lingering over the dishes, splashing in the water, lost in a daydream. What Annie did not know was the magical world that came alive as Winnie undertook the boring chores of the house.

As Winnie ran to fetch water from the rain barrels, she thought about the fairies. In a large tin tub, she mixed rain water with warm water from the kettle, and added washing soda to soften the water. Winnie remembered how old Mr. Gargin, the postman in Corbally, had entertained the girls with stories of shy fairies who often played mischievous tricks upon humans. Winnie had invented a few stories of her own and they came alive as she dipped the silverware and dishes into the washtub.

"Oh, save me, brave Winifred . . . uh, brave Evelyn," called a fork. Winnie had decided that her middle name, Evelyn, was more elegant than her first. Besides, Evelyn began with an "E," just like her older sister's name, and Winnie would do anything to be more like Emily.

The silver forks were the queen fairies with spiked shocks of hair. A wicked knife fairy had cast a spell upon the whole dish world and caused a huge storm to flood the land. Now it was up to Queen Evelyn to save the good fairies, one and all.

One by one, the dishes were drowned and then heroically rescued by Evelyn the Great. The job of washing the dishes was done in no time at all.

From the front room came the sound of Tommy tapping his wooden spoon against a kettle and Emily's soft voice chanting a nursery rhyme to his beat. Winnie smiled. Soon she'd be out the back door to play hopscotch.

"You're not done yet, Winnie," said Emily. She had come to the scullery to check on her younger sister. Her blue eyes scanned Winnie.

"Well, I've washed all the ware, and Annie says she'll dry them," said Winnie.

"Yes, but you need to come back to the mirror. Your hair hasn't been done properly," said Emily.

The Weir girls were all blessed with thick wavy hair that varied in color from Annie's dark mahogany to Emily's honey blonde. Winnie's hair was in between: chestnut brown.

"Stop pulling my hair. You're hurting me!" complained Winnie as Emily pulled a brush through her tangles.

"If you'd just sit still for one minute, we'd be done with it. You certainly are a spitfire, aren't you?" said Emily. "There now, you look like a proper British young lady," said Emily. In happier days, Ma had taught them that as citizens of Northern Ireland, they were British, proud members of the United Kingdom.

Emily braided Winnie's hair into two long ropes and tied them off with a bit of twine. With an impatient stretch of her shoulders, Winnie hopped off her perch beneath the mirror and skipped off towards the more important task of throwing pebbles onto the hopscotch pattern she and Annie had drawn in the damp soil.

Chapter 2
Of Distant Lands

"Annie, Winnie, come! Mr. Gargin's heading up our lane with the post!" Emily shouted from her stool. She set down the dirty clothes she had been scrubbing at the washboard, and stood tiptoe to watch the postman approaching.

Winnie dropped her lucky pebble into the pocket of her pinafore and peered from around the corner of the house. She had just started a game of hopscotch with Annie, but post was far more exciting.

"Come, look, Annie!" Winnie exclaimed. She spotted the postman working his way up the lane, seated atop an old bicycle. Wearing a black cape that caught the breeze and enveloped the handlebars, from a distance Mr. Gargin looked like some legendary god with dark wings. If his jerky steering were not so comical, his dark silhouette would have been rather frightening. Nonetheless, it was a big event to have the postman deliver a letter in Corbally. Winnie and Annie scrambled to the front of the house to get a better view.

As Mr. Gargin got closer, Winnie amused herself with the thought that his face resembled one of the characters from the tales he told. His protruding ears enclosed his gnome face like a set of parentheses.

"Good day to you, lasses." Mr. Gargin tipped his tweed cap as he slowly wheeled up the front yard, one hand on the handle bars. "I've got a letter for your da and ma."

"Good day to you, Mr. Gargin. Where's the letter from?" Emily stood up and shook his hand, taking the letter.

"From the looks of the stamps and the return address, it surely must have come clear across the ocean from America, lass," said Mr. Gargin.

Emily rushed to the house to deliver the letter to Ma, as she was the family letter writer.

"Dreaming about America, are you?" Mr. Gargin asked Winnie. He lifted his cap to scratch the top of his bald head.

"No, Mr. Gargin, I like it here just fine," replied Winnie.

"Well, some say the streets are paved with gold, but I don't think so. Long time ago, 'twas the dark days of the potato famine, my Uncle Paddy, he took a coffin ship, he did. Made it to New York City. Never heard from him since. Think he might have worked building those skyscraper buildings they have over there. 'Tis quite a sight to see a building tall as a mountain."

"How do you know what skyscrapers look like?" asked Winnie.

"Seen many a postcard from kin of folks 'round here. Many a lad and lass from these parts have taken off for the hope of a better life across the western sea." Mr. Gargin coughed urgently and reached for a cloth in a pocket of his cape. When he spit into the rag, Winnie politely looked away for a moment.

As he recovered, Winnie said, "Well, I'd rather stay here."

"Ay, 'tis a good home you have, though times are hard. Still not enough food and not enough work for the young lads. Suppose a pretty girl like you won't have any difficulty snaring a rich husband."

This made Winnie laugh. The thought of herself grown and married was a million years away, and of no concern to her. She suddenly remembered her parent's lessons about courtesy to elders. "Would you like to come inside for a cup of tea, Mr. Gargin?"

"No, thank you, lass. I've got a lot of ground to cover today, and the sky is threatening rain. I'd better be on my way, Miss, don't want the fairies to find me. Don't want to crush one under my wheels, you know. 'Tis very bad luck, to disturb a fairy. Must be off now. Good day to you and your family!" He kicked up his bike stand and set his bow legs on either side of the bike. Winnie watched as he wobbled his way across the front garden.

"Good day to you, Mr. Gargin!" Winnie called.

His dark triangular shape disappeared around the bend in the lane, and Winnie shivered at the thought of fairies lurking in the meadow. But today, even fairies could not keep her away from the mysterious letter.

She leapt across the front door threshold. "Emily! Annie! Who sent us the letter?" Taking a moment for her eyes to adjust to the dim interior lighting, she found Emily and Annie sitting on the edge of Ma's bed. Ma sat propped up in bed, holding the parchment stiffly, as they all huddled together, straining to read the looping writing.

Tommy circled Ma's bed yelling, "Post! Post!"

"Hush, Tommy," Emily said.

Ma held the paper close and said, "'Tis from your Aunt Mabel King in America, a town called Stamford. In a place called Connecticut." Ma unfolded the foreign-sounding names carefully on her tongue. "She visited us in Clabby several years ago."

Winnie conjured a dim memory of a stern American lady.

Ma had a faraway look as she silently read the paper. Waiting for her to speak again was unbearable. Winnie thought her heart would pop right through her chest. Finally Ma said, "Mabel says she would like to pay the passage for Emily and Annie to come and live with her. Says she could use help in her boarding house and the girls will have an opportunity for education, jobs, and maybe find a suitable American husband."

The girls exchanged startled looks with each other, unsure of how to react to this offer. Tommy, bored by this discussion, waddled out the front door to chase a barn cat.

"Ma, do we really have to go?" Annie's face reddened.

"Your Da and I will need to talk about this." Ma looked past the girls, out the tiny bedroom window. The girls knew better than to ask further. This was one of the longest conversations they had had with Ma since the scarlet fever. Ma beckoned for Emily to come closer.

"What is it, Ma?" Emily bent to put her ear near Ma's face and listened.

Winnie glanced at Annie who glared back, hugging her arms tight against her chest.

When Ma was done whispering, Emily turned to face Winnie and Annie. "Annie, you need to tend to Tommy. He's a filthy mess. Winnie, you need to deliver Da's meal to him at noon. He won't have time to break for dinner at home. Take him a picnic to share at the crossroads."

"Oh, yes!" Winnie loved the idea of picnicking with Da. She'd have him all to herself and surely there'd be a good tale to hear.

Annie stomped past her and out the door.

Before leaving the room, Winnie paused to watch Emily continue whispering with Ma. What was this secret world? She watched as Emily handed Ma a paper and pen. How Winnie wished she could read the letters Ma wrote.

Emily darted a look at Winnie, "Come now, off you go."

Winnie skipped off to gather food for herself and Da. There was a pint of milk in a ceramic jug, the heel of brown bread, and a piece of cheese, a little dry at the edge. She picked up a handful of gooseberries and laid them in a tin cup. That should make a good-enough dinner, she thought, as she placed the food in a bucket.

Since noontime was still an hour away, she searched for Annie to resume the game of hopscotch. She found Annie standing beside Emily outside near the rain barrels. Tommy was dirtier than ever, having discovered an irresistible brown mud puddle. Annie's face wore a grimace. Winnie drew nearer, listening.

"Well, I do not want to go," stated Annie.

Winnie inched closer.

"Come now, this is America we are talking about!" declared Emily, looking at her sister intently. "Annie, you are fourteen years old now, nearly a lady. Heaven knows you are as strong as an ox, and just about as stubborn, I might add. Look around you, there's no money to be made in these parts. You know as well as I that all the young people are leaving. Remember Eileen Mann and Katie Rutledge? They've all gone off to America."

"That's fine for them. . . but not me." Annie kicked a pebble and Tommy darted after it.

"I don't have to tell you that once a girl is done with the eighth class, she must find a position. You know, a servant for the upper class. Either that or go to nursing school, but Lord knows we don't have the money for that. You cannot expect to stay here forever."

"I don't care. I'd rather be a servant here than go to America." Annie set her jaw. Her dark hair framed her face like a curtain.

Emily drew in a deep breath. "Da is working his hands to the bone, and Ma's health is so poor. It's our only hope. We must obey them. What else can we do?"

"Stay right here in Corbally." Annie folded her arms defiantly.

Emily shook her head, her face softening. "I know it won't be easy at first, but Da and Ma will come along in a short while with Winnie, Tommy, and the baby. The other Weir families have all done so well. Why, Da's sister Mabel is quite an accomplished businesswoman, if her letter is to be believed. She wrote about owning five or six markets and a boarding house. Da has a lot of admiration for Mabel and her business skills. Annie, everyone knows that America is the place to make your fortune."

Annie looked around to check if anyone beside her siblings was within earshot. Satisfied that they were alone, she leaned towards Emily and said, "If America is so wonderful, why was Aunt Mabel so cross when she came to visit us?" She planted her hands upon her hips, waiting for an answer.

Emily gave a baffled shrug of her shoulders.

"You see? You can have your America. I want my Corbally!" Annie hurled a stone at a tree trunk. She stormed down the lane, her skirt whipping in the wind.

Tommy scurried to Emily's side, clutching her shins. Winnie searched Emily's face for a reaction.

Heaving a sigh, Emily led Tommy to the washtub. She dipped a rag into the water and cleaned his chubby cheeks and hands. While she tenderly wiped her brother clean, her mind seemed an ocean away.

Chapter 3
Of Clouds Above

Winnie decided to get an early start on her picnic, since Annie certainly would not be in the mood to play. She folded an old quilt, tucked it under her armpit, and lifted the tin bucket. She strolled down the lane to the crossroads. All thoughts of America evaporated in the sweet air of freshly cut hay. Winnie took in the familiar and comforting view of her family's fields and neighbor's surrounding farms. Startling green pastures littered with plump sheep. Fields of dark green leafed potato plants. Soldier-tall rows of corn stalks adjacent to lines of squat cabbage. Several cows stared at her with liquid eyes. A shoulder high hedge marked the property line, and soon she found herself at the crossroads.

Winnie had a favorite hiding spot. Under the cover of tall grass, she flattened a soft bed and pressed the quilt upon it. She lay down, staring up at the clouds. She watched the shapes float by, fascinated by how they resembled objects, then slowly transformed before her eyes. First, a chubby duckling cloud came by, but its beak drifted away from its head, and soon it looked rather like a puppy with two raised ears. She entertained herself in this manner for a quarter of an hour before she heard Da calling for her.

"Rosebud! Where are you?"

Winnie hunkered down and giggled to herself. She loved it when Da called her by this pet name. A far better name than Winnie, she thought.

"Now, where could that young girl be?" Winnie and Da often played a game of hide and seek. She suspected that Da already knew her true whereabouts, but it was more fun to go along with his game. "Let's see, Ma told me that she'd be here at high noon. From the sun overhead, she should be right about here at the crossroads, but no, she must be lost. Or maybe some roadside bandits made off with my picnic, and Rosebud is chasing them to recover my sustenance!"

Winnie couldn't stand the suspense any longer and popped up from her hideout, shouting, "I'm here, Da!"

With an exaggerated look of complete surprise, Da raised his arms above his head and said, "Thank heavens you are found! I was convinced you were off rescuing my dinner from some rogue thieves." He lifted Winnie into his arms, tossed her airborne for a split second and caught her with a hug.

"Oh, Da, you knew I was here all along," Winnie laughed.

"Looks to me as if you've been taking a nap out here," Da said. He dropped down onto the quilt looking tired and flushed, with dirt and hay seed filling the creases of his skin and clothing. When his eyes met Winnie's expectant face, his mouth spread into a contagious grin, exposing his large teeth.

"No, Da, I haven't been sleeping at all. I've been watching the clouds. You see, up there." Winnie pointed overhead. "There's a cloud that looks like a hunchback. See his cap, and the sack he's carrying?"

Da squinted, scrutinizing the sky, then his eyes grew wide. "Why, Rosebud, I do believe your hunchback is not a hunchback at all! 'Tis the one and only Finn MacCool! And that's not a sack, 'tis a lump of earth he's about to hurl at his foe."

"Oh, Da, tell me the story!"

Da cleared his throat and began his tale. "Yes, as you may know, Finn MacCool was a famous giant in Ireland. But did you know that he had a rival across the Irish Sea in my homeland of Scotland?"

"No!" Winnie sat bolt upright.

"Well, Finn caught wind of what this Scottish giant was saying about him. The Scottish giant went by the name of Angus. You see, Angus was mocking Finn, questioning his power of prophesy and his strength. So, as you might imagine, Finn grew quite angry. He hurled a huge rock across the sea to Scotland as a challenge to Angus."

"What did Angus do?" Winnie sidled closer to Da.

"He did what every natural born giant would do, he threw a message back in a rock. He told Finn that since it is a well-known fact that giants are not swimmers, he would not be able to face him in the challenge across the sea.

"Well, Finn was not inclined to let off Angus quite so easily. He used his brute strength to wrench apart chunks of rock that were part of the coastline, and he stood each rock upright, much like a pillar. He worked at this until he had formed a causeway from Ireland to Scotland. Now Angus had no excuse."

"Did Angus use the causeway to come across?"

"Yes, that he did. But Finn was prepared for Angus. He got himself dressed up as a baby."

"A giant baby?!" Winnie exploded into giggles, collapsing onto the quilt, rolling over and giggling some more.

"Yes, and do you know what this giant baby did when Angus came to Finn's house?"

"Did he ask Angus to fetch him a bottle of milk?" Winnie propped herself up with her elbows, eager to hear the conclusion.

"No, Finn bit Angus' hand! This took him completely by surprise, and when Angus gathered his wits to run away, Finn was out of his cradle, chasing him across the causeway. Finn scooped out lumps of earth and hurled them at Angus. One particular lump was so huge, it left behind a great loch, Loch Neagh, to be exact."

"I know Loch Neagh from my geography lessons. 'Tis the largest loch in Ireland, located within four counties: Antrim, Armagh, Derry, and our very own, Tyrone."

"My, you certainly have been paying attention in your geography lessons, Rosebud! 'Twas that very same loch. And unfortunately for Finn, he missed Angus, and the lump of earth landed in the sea. The lump formed an island. Do you know which one that might be?"

"Now let me guess . . . an island off the north coast of Ireland. Would it be the Isle of Man?"

"My Rosebud is absolutely brilliant in geography! Yes, 'tis the very same island. And one day when we get enough money, we'll go take a train ride for a holiday to see the Giant's Causeway."

"Oh, Da, could we?"

"All in good time." Da sighed. His rugged face looked tired. "I've worked up quite an appetite with this cloud watching. What have you brought me today, Rosebud?"

Winnie set out her picnic and they munched on the dry bread and cheese. A cloud passed over the sun and darker thoughts of losing Emily and Annie to a strange country cast a momentary shadow. Winnie took a long drink of milk, trying to wash away unhappy thoughts.

"You are the finest picnic-maker in all of the British Kingdom, Rosebud," Da said, as he scooped up a handful of gooseberries and handed them to her.

"Thank you." Winnie grinned, taking the berries. The sun broke out and all thoughts of this afternoon's post dissolved. She drank in the afternoon as if it could last forever.

Chapter 4
I Rest Me in the Thought

The next day, just as Ma had promised, a decision about America had been made.

"Come now, Annie, Winnie, Tommy! Dinner's ready!" Emily called. She stood before the table as Ma lowered herself onto a spot on the bench. Da came through the back door and hung up his cap.

Winnie looked up at the clock on a shelf near the hearth. It was already one o'clock, the family's customary time for dinner. The morning had flown by. She came to the table a bit more slowly than her usual pace. She searched Ma and Da's face for a clue. Was there an extra strain across Da's brow?

Annie lifted Tommy into his tall chair and tried to arrange his wee legs that just wouldn't stay still. Emily set out the small pot of boiled potatoes and vegetables she'd prepared, and the family sat down.

"Keep still and fold your hands, Tommy," Annie said, a little too sharply.

Da started a prayer. Winnie listened warily. Was his voice quaking a bit? When he finished, he glanced over at Ma. She nodded her head.

Da set his hands across the table and cupped them atop Annie and Emily's. He said, "Now girls, your mother and I have given this idea of going to America a lot of thought, even before Mabel's letter. We have come to the decision that America holds much more promise for the Weir family. Given Mabel's generous offer, we will start by sending Emily and Annie first. Ma, Winnie, Tommy, and I will come after the baby is born . . . and, after we gather enough money for the passage."

Annie pursed her lips, and Emily shifted in her seat.

"'Twill be hard for you to leave, but it is the right thing to do," Da said, his eyes moist but hopeful.

Tommy ate his potatoes with great relish and cried out, "More! More!" Hushing him, Emily slipped some of her stew onto his platter. She asked, "When are we to go?"

Da said, "Mabel will purchase your tickets for passage on a grand steamship called The California. Departs from Londonderry on October 9. That's about two months from now."

Emily straightened her back and said, "If this is your decision, I shall abide by it, Da." Everyone shifted their eyes expectantly to Annie.

"Must I go?" she asked in a small voice, her face twisted.

Winnie watched Ma stiffen as she turned towards Annie and said, "Surely, you will go." Surprised at Ma's sudden burst of resolve, Winnie wondered if Ma thought that all of their problems, including the scarlet fever and William's death, were because they were so poor here in Corbally.

Da squeezed Annie's hand. "Yes, you will go, and you will work hard. Before you know it, we'll be together in America. Life is difficult at times, but there will be rewards. America has opportunity, and we shall all benefit in the end."

Emily stared at her plate and nibbled a few small forkfuls of stew.

Annie pushed a mound of potatoes back and forth across her plate.

Winnie pierced a turnip and slipped it into her mouth, but her throat was so tight, she could barely swallow.

Finally, Annie set her fork aside her plate and said briskly, "Excuse me." No one dared remind her of her chores. She left through the back door.

"Let me help you to your room, Isabella," Da said as Ma turned to rise. He walked Ma to the bedroom.

Emily lifted Tommy out of his chair. "Come with me to the scullery, Tommy." Winnie could hear him pounding a spoon against an empty tub as Emily busied herself with the dirty ware.

Still sitting all alone at the table, Winnie stroked the worn empty places on the bench where her sisters had sat.

After a few moments, Emily peeked in and said, "Winnie, I'll finish washing up. Why don't you go find Annie? She's been gone a bit too long. I think she went that way down the lane."

Winnie nodded. A brisk walk down the lane was exactly what she needed. She blinked back tears. Soon she'd be losing her sisters. And how could she possibly take on the responsibilities of the house the way Emily had?

Emily had pointed in the direction of Clabby. Winnie ran down the lane.

After about a mile with no sign of Annie, she spotted the vast groomed pastures that belonged to Grandda Moffatt, Ma's father. Born into a family of wealthy land-owners, Ma had given up her inheritance to marry Da. Da had tried to explain it to Winnie, but it really didn't make much sense. Grandda Moffatt didn't seem to like the Weirs since Da was Scottish. Da had said that Ma and the Weirs were "disowned."

A rustling in some hedges made Winnie start. Peering over the tops of the bushes, she noticed shiny dark hair.

"Don't follow me," Annie said, squatting low in the hedgerow.

"What are you doing here?" Winnie asked.

"I want to be alone. That's all." Annie hunched down lower.

"Well, you'd better come home soon. Da is expecting you to help him in the fields this afternoon." Winnie turned to leave. She understood the need to be alone.

"Winnie, wait!" Annie rose from the hedge and beckoned her.

"What is it?" Winnie moved closer.

Annie pulled her behind the hedge and pointed to the Moffatt plantation. "Did you know that Ma used to have a rose garden when she was a little girl?"

"No."

"That's why Da gave her that yellow rosebush to plant in front of our house. Da said that yellow roses stood for joy, and he wanted Ma to feel joy in the new house."

"I didn't know that." Winnie smiled. She loved thinking about Ma and Da in happier moments.

"And there's a pond over there." Annie pointed beyond the large house. "Ma used to tell us stories about a dozen white swans floating on that pond."

"How lovely." Winnie looked at Annie's tear streaked face.

"Grandda clipped the swan's wings so they wouldn't fly away."

"Oh," Winnie said, flinching at the thought.

"And when Ma was a girl, Grandda wouldn't let her play with the Catholic children," Annie said.

"Why not?" Winnie asked. There were plenty of Catholic children at school, and as far as she could tell they behaved like all children. Some good, some naughty, but there wasn't any particular Protestant or Catholic behavior she could discern.

"Don't know. Just forbid it. Just the way he forbid Ma to marry Da."

"I'm glad Da doesn't treat us like that," Winnie said. Just as the words escaped from her mouth she realized this might not be the right thing to say at the moment.

Annie's eyes welled up with tears and she heaved a sob. "Winnie, if he loves us so much, why is he making us leave?"

"But Da says we'll all be together, soon enough," Winnie said, patting Annie's back. Winnie reached into her pocket and handed her sister a handkerchief.

They lingered for a moment in their hedgerow hide-out. Overhead a v-shaped flock of geese flew by, their honking loud and dissonant. Winnie watched them soar through the clouds and said, "Sometimes I fancy that I could fly like those geese."

"Oh, Winnie, you can be a goose, but I fancy the swan," Annie said.

Winnie considered this in silence. She definitely wouldn't want to have her wings clipped. Finally, she said, "We should be going back now."

Annie nodded and they wound their way back up the lane without speaking.

Arriving at the farm, Annie pulled away. "I'm going up to the house to wash my face. Would you tell Da I'll be there soon?"

"Of course." Winnie nodded. Annie seemed calmer. Maybe she wasn't so against the idea of America. Just then, Winnie caught sight of Da moving sacks of feed from the back of a cart to the barn. As she got closer she noticed him struggling with a particularly tall sack of grain. He made an awkward movement, and reached both his hands to his chest. Pausing to catch his breath, he turned to smile at her.

"Let me help you with that," she called.

Emily, who was shaking out a rug at the doorway, grinned at Winnie. "You'd haul an entire wagon of peat for Da if he asked, wouldn't you, Winnie?"

"Of course I need your help, Rosebud. Hurry now, you know how I cannot get through a day without one of our tale-tellings."

Winnie clambered aboard the back of the cart, giggling in anticipation of another lively story.

"Tell me the story of when you first met Ma," begged Winnie, handing Da a burlap sack of grain.

"Ah, my favorite tale!" Da coughed and patted his chest. "Well, as you know, my home country is Scotland, just twenty miles east across the sea. Since my luck was down in Scotland, I decided to try my hand at shopkeeping in Ireland, before setting out for my final destination of America. I set up my shop, and wouldn't you know, 'twasn't but a week went by and your Ma, Isabella, came waltzin' in with her Da, Mr. Moffatt. You see, she was a school teacher in Bristol. That's in England, as you know. She was a princess, your Ma. All fancy in her traveling clothes, a shawl across her shoulders. Her Da, now he was all proper and stuffy. Wouldn't let his daughter out of his sight. She was on holiday from teaching, paying a visit to the family homestead in Clabby. Wouldn't you know, she lived right next to my shop? They were just coming by to get some provisions, I suppose, for their evening tea and such. Well, I saw your Ma give me a glance, and that was enough for me."

"Tell me the part about her eyes, Da." Winnie sat on the edge of the wagon motionless, for fear of missing a single word.

"Oh, yes, her eyes. The Weirs have the blue, but your Ma, she had the darkest deepest brown, that set me soaring to the clouds. If I was a swearing man, I'd swear she could see my soul with those deep eyes." Da's eyes looked far away, as if he were transported back to another time without worry, without the scarlet fever.

"Anyway, she pretended she hadn't noticed me, but I could tell. There was a force between us that even her uppity Da could not break. Next day, she came in to buy some peat, so she said. I knew better. She came to have a look at my handsome face!" Da chuckled.

"When did you ask her to marry you?" Winnie asked, although she already knew the answer.

"Well, 'twas a fortnight later, when she was preparing to return to Bristol. I knew she was going because she was purchasing some biscuits to eat on the long coach ride back to the boat across the sea. I said to her, 'Now, you make sure you come back here next holiday.' Says she, coy and sweet, 'Why would I want to do a thing like that?' I think she nearly fell over when I replied, 'Why, to marry me, of course!'"

"You didn't!" exclaimed Winnie, relishing the climax of this familiar tale. She loved to imagine her mother spirited, young, happy.

"Course, I did, and of course, she blushed. I'll never forget those bonny brown eyes looking into mine, checking to see if I was sincere. She got her answer right away. She knew I could not tease about such powerful feelings. Said she'd ask her Da. We both knew her Da would not approve of me. A Scotsman, no less. But I also knew she'd come back to marry me." Da smiled at the memory.

"Ah, she gave up a lot for love. Her Da, he did not allow the marriage, and so when your Ma ran off to marry me, he disowned her. No inheritance from the family fortune or the like. Acted cold as stone each time he passed us on the lane. But your Ma, she knew a true treasure when she saw one." Da beamed in pride. "We married for love, and that was not the way for old man Moffatt. Your Ma has no regrets, what with you and her three other treasures. She has love and family. What more could a British princess want?"

Winnie wished she could believe that Ma was so happy. But the disowning seemed to have worn hard on her. And the scarlet fever. And losing William.

"There's one more part to this story I've never told you, Rosebud," Da added.

"What's that, Da?"

"These treasures of your Ma and Da, you see, they are too precious to lie idle here in Ireland. No chance to shine here. These children will go off to a land of riches and gold, a land of opportunity where they can be brilliant."

"Do you mean America?" Winnie's eyes widened as she hung onto every word Da uttered.

"Yes, America is the place for the Weirs. It has always been my goal to settle in America. In good time, we'll all go over and make our mark in this world. My brothers and sisters have gone before me. Each and every one of them has made a small fortune. It's our turn next."

Da's smile faded to a slight frown as a wave of pain crossed his chest.

Winnie asked, "Da, what's wrong?"

"Oh, nothing more than a bit of indigestion. My Rosebud must be feeding Clucky such fine grain, that's all. Clucky's eggs are too rich for my Scottish blood." Da laughed and dismissed Winnie's concern with a wave of his hand.

"You know, your Ma does not deserve to live the way she does. In America a young lady can marry for love and would not be punished for it. I want the best for my family, and America is the answer." Da punched the air for emphasis. He said, "I suppose it's time we got back to work." Patting the large pockets of his jacket and asked, "But first, a sweet for my Rosebud?"

Winnie nodded enthusiastically and popped the candy into her mouth.

"Thanks, Da." She hugged him, taking in his scent of wool, turf fire, and the earth. She'd be happy anywhere in the world, as long as Da was there, too.

Chapter 5
The Lord Is King, Let the Heavens Ring
The Church of Ireland
Clabby, County Tyrone

A week before Annie and Emily's departure, a rush of autumn air blew through a crack in the girls' bedroom window. Winnie awoke, and then pulled a quilt over her head. It was too cold to fetch the water!

"Up you go, Winnie," urged Emily. She was seated upon a wooden stool beside the bed, pulling on her Sunday stockings.

"It can't be time to get up!" Resigned, Winnie threw off the covers and made a dash to the closet to grab a frock before the chill air had a chance to get at her. She wiggled into her clothes and rummaged in the bureau for a sweater.

"It's porridge for breakfast today. But if you want some toast, you can make it for yourself." Emily dipped her head to get a quick view of her face in the bureau mirror. She cupped some water in her hands from a basin and rubbed the sleep from her face. She stood to leave the room, her Sunday dress unfurling from her lap and swishing gracefully as she strode across the floor. A true princess, thought Winnie.

With old black shoes on her feet, Winnie threw an itchy hand-knit sweater over her frock and ran out the back door. She'd change into her Sunday best after the messy chores were done. Making a brief stop at the outhouse, she proceeded to check on the hens, and to fill a bucket of water at the well.

Once the water had been delivered to Annie, Winnie was overwhelmed with hunger. Last night's meal of potatoes and carrots was rather skimpy. Toast with strawberry jam would be very nice, she thought. She went to the scullery to slice a thick cut of bread. Sawing through the dry loaf, she was disappointed at the stale bread, but she knew it could be worse. There had been many mornings without bread. Holding it above some glowing embers, Winnie was mesmerized by the warmth of the fire and the dancing flames.

Annie joined Winnie, toasting her bread a bit lighter than Winnie's preferred dark toast. Tommy scampered in from Ma and Da's bedroom looking sleepy and rosy cheeked.

"Come and have a seat with me, Tommy." Winnie patted her lap. She swallowed hard. In a little over a week, she and Tommy would be the only children left. Tommy sat for a brief moment, but pulled away.

"Emmie, Emmie, eat!" He trotted to the scullery where Emily was mixing some frothy milk into a pot of porridge.

"You certainly have a keen sense of smell, Tommy. You smelled the porridge clear across the house. Woke you up from sweet dreams." Emily patted the top of her brother's head.

Ma entered the main room and eased herself onto the bench. Winnie brought over a kettle of hot water and poured her some tea. "How are you feeling today, Ma?" she asked, peering into Ma's remote face.

"Been better," Ma answered, scraping the sugar bowl for any last crystals of sugar.

As Winnie continued pouring cups of tea for each family member, she thought: how will I ever take care of Ma and Tommy the way Emily does?

Da came in through the back door. "Morning, my dear family!" Sitting next to Ma, he rubbed her back up and down, "You're looking fine this morning Isabella. Have you got the strength to go to church with the rest of us?"

"No, not today."

"You just need more rest, that's all, Isabella. Rest and a better climate in America. Yes, that's how we'll cure you."

After Da's morning prayer, they dipped their spoons into the porridge. Annie and Winnie crunched on their toast.

"Have you girls heard the story of the Darby boys down the lane?" Da asked.

"John," Ma shook her head in disapproval.

"The story is all over town. Winnie will hear it at school tomorrow, so we all might as well hear it first from the most reliable source of all!" Da chuckled, wiping milk from his mustache with an old cloth.

"Tell it please, Da," Winnie begged.

"Da, Da, Da!" Tommy banged his spoon against his bowl and splattered some porridge across the table. Annie used a rag to wipe up the mess and directed Tommy's spoon into his mouth.

"I'll tell it, if it's all right with Ma . . ." Da met Ma's eyes, and she gave a resigned shrug.

"Well, seems the boys had been indulging in every schoolchild's after school habit. They were helping themselves to a taste of a farmer's crop. 'Twas turnips, I believe. Farmer's name was Doohan. You see, they'd sneak into Doohan's pasture on the way home from school, dig up a plump turnip, smash it on a stone, and eat it the best way: raw and dirty!"

Winnie and her sisters exchanged looks and giggled at the thought of the dirty mouthed Darby boys, a welcome diversion from talk of the journey to America.

Tommy snickered, "Dirty, dirty, eat dirt!"

"Not only did they take a few too many extra turnips for the sheer fun of smashing them, they took their prank a mite too far. You see, when Doohan chased them away with his hoe, the boys thought they had a right to take whatever they pleased. They figured they'd play a prank on Doohan. Put him in his place. As if Doohan wouldn't know who the mischief makers might be!" Da stirred his teacup. Adding a splash of cream, he paused for a sip.

"The Darby boys waited for the cover of dusk and sneaked into Doohan's orchard. They dismantled his wagon and hung the wheels from a tree like ornaments. I suppose young boys find this sort of thing to be amusing, but what would I know, an old man myself?" Da laughed, as Ma shook her head.

"As you might imagine, Doohan did not see the humor in this! The next afternoon, those Darby boys boldly returned to admire their handiwork. Doohan was no fool. He lay in wait until the boys were high up in the boughs of his most prized pear tree. Then, he released a fearsome bull into the paddock. The bull circled the tree, snorting his displeasure at the intruders for the better part of that afternoon and night. Poor Mrs. Darby! Was she ever worried. After a sleepless night, with no boys returning home from school, she traced their path from home to school. Hearing the boy's cries from the tree, she pleaded with Doohan to release the boys to her custody. Needless to say, you won't be finding any more schoolchildren in Doohan's pastures!" Da tipped the remaining tea from his cup into his mouth and added, "Now, if my Rosebud ever gets the urge to have an after school snack, I'd suggest she find more friendly pastures."

Ma said, "That's enough, John."

Da said, "Ah, girls, have a look at the clock. 'Tis getting late."

"Da, please tell us another story," Annie said, settling deeper into her seat.

"There's no more time, love. Now let's wash up." Da helped raise Ma to her feet.

Winnie lingered at her spot and wondered why Annie wasn't getting up.

Emily called from the scullery, "Come, now, Annie, help me wash up." She dipped her head through the doorway and added, "Winnie, you need to put on your church clothes. And make sure your hands are clean, fingernails as well!" In the old days, Ma would line up the children at the doorway for inspection. Proper church attire included polished shoes, best dresses, and Sunday bonnets. Emily had taken over the position of Sunday inspector.

"Oh, Tommy, you've got porridge everywhere, including behind your ears!" Emily took Tommy by the hand and pulled him to the tub outside for a good cleaning. Annie trudged to the scullery balancing a pile of dirty dishes.

Winnie hurried off to her room to change. When she was done, she overheard voices in the scullery. Tiptoeing closer, she eavesdropped from behind a cupboard.

"But Da, I don't care about opportunity. I want to stay here with you and Ma. I'm not ready to be a young lady." From the tone of Annie's voice, Winnie could tell that she was near tears.

"Ah, my dear Annie, I know how you must feel. But you cannot possibly understand how this place has nothing to offer you. America has hope and possibility. And we'll all come over as soon as we save the fare for the rest of us."

"But Da, what if Aunt Mabel is . . . What if she's, well, not like you and Ma?" Annie's voice reached a shrill pitch.

"Annie, Mabel is my sister. She went off to America when I was just a young lad, and she has done so well. And what a business sense she has. To think, a woman can run a market and own property! The Weirs believe in hard work and education, but Ireland is a dead end." Winnie peeked out from behind the cupboard and saw Da rest his hand on Annie's shoulder.

"But, I don't want to leave you and Ma!" Tears streamed down Annie's face, and Da's posture softened.

"There, there, 'twill be all right. You'll see, everything has a way of working out." He stroked her dark hair. "At church today, you will need to ask God for strength. We all need God's help through these difficult times." Da hugged Annie and Winnie thought she saw a tear roll down Da's cheek. Suddenly she felt embarrassed at spying on such a private scene.

Da stepped through the threshold and glanced at the clock. "Have a look at the time, girls. 'Tis time to leave for church!" As Winnie emerged from her hiding spot, he looked at her curiously, then winked. "Have you passed your inspection yet, Rosebud?"

"Not yet." Winnie reached upward to straighten her crooked bonnet, and rearranged the loose strands of hair escaping from her braids. Last night was bath night and her freshly washed hair was especially unruly. She trotted off to the bedroom to fix herself in the mirror before lining up at the front door. Coming back to the door, she took a place in between Annie and Tommy.

Emily surveyed the children, imitating Ma's scrutiny. "Annie, you look lovely. I like the new lace you added onto the sleeves of your blouse." Emily brushed the fine stitches with her fingertip. Emily and Annie both knew that it had been mostly Emily's handiwork. She was teaching both Annie and Winnie how to crochet lace, but no one could match her fine work.

"Now, Tommy, I've just washed you, so you should be fine, if you could just steer clear of the puddles in the lane." Emily looked at Winnie. "Now, how's my Winnie today?" Winnie could feel her sister's critical eye roving over her body, searching for a smudge, a wrinkle, a speck. "Well, if you'd just smooth out your hair, you'd be a perfect angel." Emily's stern expression gave way to a smile as Winnie used a lick of spit to keep her frizzy hair together at the ends of her braids. They waited for Da to come back from the bedroom where he was plumping a pillow for Ma's sore back.

Da joined them, buttoning up his overcoat and tossing a scarf across his shoulders. Winnie copied him with a theatrical toss of her own scarf.

"Look how Winnie imitates Da," Annie said sharply. Winnie wondered if she was jealous.

"Yes, if ever there was a pair made for each other, 'tis Winnie and Da," Emily laughed. Winnie's mood lightened, knowing that on Sunday she'd have plenty of time with Da.

They walked down the lane together in the light rain of the morning, taking in the green pastures and the straight edge of the hedges that ran alongside them. Creeping ivy nearly smothered ancient beech trees. Everyone concentrated on taking careful steps between puddles, the better to keep their Sunday shoes shiny. Breathing deeply, cheeks flushed from the vigorous walk, Winnie thought how wonderful it felt to be together. If only Ma were here too.

After two miles, the old stone church came into view. Its pointed spire housed a bell that rang deeply, reverberating in Winnie's chest. A small crowd of townspeople had gathered at the front steps. Since Da had special responsibilities as a member of the vestry, he headed inside, ahead of the rest, to prepare for the service.

Emily led the way up the aisle to a pew near the front. The sanctuary smelled of damp wool and burning coal from the stove that kept the church barely warm. Da slipped in alongside Annie just as the service began. Winnie watched as Annie and Emily prayed silently. Annie quietly sniffled and wiped her nose with a handkerchief from her pocket. Da patted her hand.

Winnie bowed her head and asked God for the strength to do her duties once her sisters were gone. Tommy sat as still as could be expected, occupying himself with a handful of pebbles he'd pillaged from the church path.

Then Da stepped forward to the pulpit. "Let us now read from the Gospel according to Luke 10:38-42."

Winnie noticed his voice break ever so slightly.

> *Now as they went on their way, he entered a certain village, where a woman named Martha welcomed him into her home. She had a sister named Mary, who sat at the Lord's feet and listened to what he was saying. But Martha was distracted by her many tasks; so she came to him and asked, 'Lord, do you not care that my sister has left me to do all the work by myself? Tell her then to help me.' But the Lord answered her, 'Martha, Martha, you are worried and distracted by many things; there is need of only one thing. Mary has chosen the better part, which will not be taken away from her.'*

Stepping down to the pews, Da didn't seem to be able to make eye contact with his daughters, for fear of losing his composure.

The piano broke into a joyous refrain, signaling the end of the service, and the worshippers greeted each other, sharing conversation and news. The buzz of voices seemed to lift Da's somber mood.

"Girls, I'd like you to meet a lady who will be traveling to America on the very same ship as you. Mr. Gargin told me just last week. Her name is Lizzie Askin. Her Da's got a farm across town. The two used to come to my shop in Clabby. I'll introduce you to her." Da beckoned them to come down the aisle to greet a tall, strong-boned woman who was standing beside an older man, her father. "Come along, children, follow your Da."

"Lizzie Askin, so glad to see you this morning!" Da gave a hearty handshake and Lizzie nodded and smiled, apparently recognizing him from years past.

"So good to see you again, Mr. Weir," she said.

"Miss Askin, have you met my children?" Lizzie held out her hand to Emily as Da introduced them.

"Pleased to meet you, Emily. And the other two girls must be your sisters. John was always carrying on about his three beautiful daughters." Lizzie laughed, holding out her hand to greet Annie and Winnie.

"Yes! This is Annie. She and Emily will be on the ship together with you next week." Da smiled.

"And you must be Winnie. I guess I won't have much of a chance to get to know you as well. It's a good thing your Da has told me so much about you already. And of course, here's wee Tommy." Lizzie gave Winnie a solid handshake and patted the top of Tommy's head. She motioned to her own father.

"Let me introduce you to my father, Richard Askin." Mr. Askin was a craggy old man, who looked as if he had shrunken from his previously large stature to a hunched-over version of himself. Beneath the wrinkles of his face, his dark eyes twinkled merrily.

"Lovely service today," he said. "Would you like a sweet, lass?" He pulled a butterscotch stick out of his pocket and offered it to Winnie.

"Thank you, Mr. Askin," Winnie said, happily unwrapping the candy from the waxed paper.

Mr. Askin stooped to offer Tommy a sweet. Tommy grabbed it a little too hastily, and everyone laughed at his lapse of manners. He ran down the church path, dangerously close to mud puddles. Emily and Annie bustled after him.

The adults began to discuss topics that were of no interest to Winnie. Weather, crops, taxes, the troubles stirring in the south. Relishing the rich taste of butterscotch, she started to daydream. What if she and her sisters were to run away? Instead of going to America, they could stowaway here in the church. They'd make their beds in the choir balcony. Winnie would go to the front altar and talk to God. She had so many questions. She'd ask Him why He let her brother William die. At five years old, he really hadn't much of a chance to live. And why had Grandda disowned her family? Why was Ma so full of aches and always so tired? Why did her sisters need to leave Corbally? Winnie closed her eyes and tried to imagine the face of God. That's strange, she thought: God looks just like Da with a long white beard. Of course, they could never run away.

Winnie's daydream was interrupted by the sound of laughter from the adults. Tommy had just been returned by Emily and Annie, looking quite disheveled. His hands were muddy and he had a slash of dirt across his forehead. He seemed perfectly happy with this state of filth.

"So then, Lizzie, I want to thank you from the bottom of my heart," Da said. "The girls will look for you when they arrive by train at the Londonderry docks. It is very reassuring to know that you'll be watching out for them until they are united with Mabel on the other side."

Lizzie and her father took leave, and Da gathered Tommy into his arms. "It's off to the washtub with you! Two baths in one day . . . you'll be the cleanest lad in all of the British Kingdom!"

They took off down the lane, Emily wrapped her arm around Annie's and prattled on about what Lizzie had told her. "And Lizzie says her best friend, Sarah, left two years ago and has written to tell her all about the journey. Lizzie will be joining Sarah in Brooklyn to work as a servant."

Annie was very quiet.

Winnie kept pace with Da, who was telling Tommy a tale from the Bible about Noah, his ark, and all the animals he saved.

"With all the rain we get here in Ireland, sometimes I get a hankering to build myself an ark," Da said.

"Da! Make ark!" Tommy's face lit up.

"I'll do something even better. One day, Tommy, you'll be getting on a steamship as large as Noah's ark. 'Twill be full of people from all over the world heading to a promised land. Just wait . . . one day, there'll be an ark for Tommy and Winnie."

Chapter 6
Of Rocks and Trees

The next morning, Emily called from the hearth, "Winnie, come! It's time we left for school." It was Monday, the worst day of the week. And to think, her sisters would be gone in just seven days. She fastened the last button of her school dress.

Winnie grabbed her satchel full of writing tablets and textbooks, and picked up a lunch bucket from the table. Emily had prepared her lunch, and Winnie was glad to see a pear, a jam sandwich, and a half pint of milk.

Emily cradled a bunch of kindling to donate to the school hearth. She said, "Annie, 'tis time for Winnie to be off. Are you going with her, or do you want to stay behind and mind Tommy?"

Annie's sleepy face appeared at the doorway. "I'm not ready. You'd best go without me this morning. I'll mind Tommy."

"All right, but Da will be expecting you to help him with the new calf this morning." Emily motioned to Winnie to come.

Winnie kissed Ma and Tommy goodbye, and joined Emily. The

first mile was a straight stretch of farm pastures. Along the narrow lane, yellow buds peeked out from spiky gorse bushes. Gnarled hawthorn hedges marked off fields of crops. Fat trees dripped in ivy, like melted wax on candle sticks. A view of the small rectangular stone building appeared at the bend in the lane, smoke rising from its chimney. Several classmates began to overtake Winnie and Emily on the lane. A red-haired boy sneaked up behind Winnie, tugged her braid hard, and ran ahead, laughing.

"I'd chase you, Connor Quinn, if it weren't for this bundle!" She'd remember to get back at Connor at lunchtime. The sound of unfamiliar deep laughter from behind made Winnie look over her shoulder.

"I think my little brother fancies you," said a taller boy, almost a man, who grinned mischievously. He was Connor's brother, Owen.

"Not likely," Winnie answered, blushing, then realized Owen wasn't paying attention to her anymore. His eyes lingered on Emily.

"Winnie, you'd better move along. 'Tis nearly time for school to begin." Emily laid the kindling down at the woodpile and joined Owen for the walk back home. Winnie wondered if Emily liked Owen.

Once inside, Winnie sat down upon a bench in a large classroom with students of ages ranging from four years old to thirteen. She smiled as her classmate, Hannah Curran, hurried in. The nine o'clock bell chimed, and the teacher entered the room. All of the students stood and said in unison, "Good morning, Miss Whivisty."

"Good morning, children. You may be seated."

Several of the youngest students were still struggling with the buttons on their overcoats, so Miss Whivisty asked Winnie and Hannah to assist them in the back of the room at the coat closet while she took the roll call. One by one, Miss Whivisty called out a student's name and each stood up, saying, "Present, Ma'am."

Whispering in the coat closet as they squeezed wooden buttons through the openings of wee overcoats, Winnie said, "Hannah, 'tis just one week till Annie and Emily leave for America." The words hung in the air, still unbelievable even though she herself had said them.

"Oh, you'll miss them sorely, I suppose," Hannah said.

"Yes. You'll come 'round and play with me sometimes?"

"Of course," Hannah answered. Winnie hung the last overcoat on a hook on the wall, nodded to the youngster to return to his seat, and glanced up at Miss Whivisty.

"We will begin our lessons, with close attention to the sixth class review. As you know, the inspectors will be coming next Monday, and we all need to work especially hard at memorizing our lessons." Winnie and Hannah silently slipped back onto the school bench. "The rest of you shall work on your penmanship lessons, and I will come 'round to check. Remember, speak only in quiet voices."

Miss Whivisty circulated about the room as students worked at various lessons. Her wavy red hair was pulled up to the top of her head in a loose bun. A few corkscrew tendrils strayed down the back of her neck.

Winnie hoped to eavesdrop on the sixth class review, the better to succeed when she graduated to that level next year. While she did her fifth class penmanship lesson, she could hear their geography lesson. Mrs. Whivisty's voice listed the thirty-two counties of Ireland, the population, the landmarks, and buildings of significance. How could Miss Whivisty act as if this were an ordinary day? Didn't she know that the whole world would be tipped upside down next week?

Arithmetic followed penmanship. Winnie dutifully calculated Miss Whivisty's problems from the blackboard. If only she could do her numbers as quickly as Emily. Next, it was time for story writing. Winnie struggled to write her piece about a princess who was locked inside an enchanted castle. An evil witch had enslaved the princess, forcing her to toil away each day in solitude. While the picture in her mind was quite vivid, the words lay flat and lifeless on the paper before her.

"Students, dinner will be in five minutes, so please put away your papers. Before we break, I would like to review the rules for the school yard." There was a murmur of shuffling papers and benches squeaking against the stone floor. "Now, who would like to remind the class of our outdoor rules?" Miss Whivisty surveyed the class as several hands shot up.

"Yes, Mary?" Miss Whivisty addressed a round faced girl with wavy black hair.

"When you play, be sure you hurt no one."

"Yes, very good, and what else?" Miss Whivisty watched as several more hand sprung up, and she chose Connor.

"Don't throw stones," Connor said sheepishly, as he realized he had been guilty of this crime more than a few time.

"Most certainly not! Anything else?" Miss Whivisty noticed Winnie's hand and called on her.

"Be courteous, especially to your elders." Winnie flushed as all eyes fell upon her.

"Well said, Winnie." Miss Whivisty piled some books into a tidy stack atop her desk and looked up to check the clock. As it was twelve o'clock noon, she pulled the rope of the bell. Finally, the long-awaited sound of the lunch bell rang.

Winnie hadn't forgotten Connor's challenge to her on the lane in front of school earlier that morning. Once outdoors, she yelled, "I'm 'It'!" Her classmates scattered in all directions, running at top speed. Winnie dug into the grass with her old black shoes and was right on Connor's heels. He turned a panicky face to her and tried his best to dodge her outstretched hand, but he was not quick enough.

"Got you!" Winnie shouted triumphantly. In an instant, Connor changed directions and pursued another classmate who wasn't quite as swift as Winnie.

"Winnie! I've saved you a seat on the wall over here." Hannah pointed to a spot beside her.

"I'll be right there." Winnie scooted to her perch beside Hannah and hungrily pulled out her jam sandwich. It was gone in no time, and the milk vanished just as quickly. She savored each bite of the ripe pear, even chewed through the core and seeds to get every last bit of the sweet fruit. She wiped the juice from her face and licked each finger. She could have eaten five more pears. Winnie hopped off the wall. "Hannah, let's go play some more tag."

After a quarter of an hour of vigorous running, the school bell chimed, signaling students to return for the afternoon lessons. The fifth class had a spelling test to complete, then crocheting lessons. Hannah's family had supplied the school with some wool, the sheep having been shorn last week. Winnie was a bit frustrated by her uneven stitches. Emily's crocheting never looked so lumpy.

"Let's have a look at your blanket," Hannah said. She set her yarn and needle upon her lap and looked at Winnie's handiwork. "Ma says, 'Keep a firm tension as you feed the thread.'"

Winnie shrugged. Today she had much bigger things to think about than crocheting.

The end of the day did not come soon enough. The three o'clock bell chimed for dismissal and the younger students shot out the door like steam from a kettle. It was Winnie and Hannah's turn to stay after to sweep out the coat closet. Connor swabbed the school floor with a damp mop, silently brooding after his embarrassing defeat in tag at lunch. Miss Whivisty chatted with some parents out in the schoolyard.

After a few minutes had gone by, Emily and Annie appeared at the school doorway and called, "Winnie, are you finished yet?"

"Yes, let me get my coat and bucket, and I'll be on my way." Hastily propping the brooms in the closet, Winnie and Hannah pulled on their coats and grabbed their things, leaving Connor to finish his job.

Hannah waved as she left in the opposite direction.

"Was that your friend, Connor, mopping the floor?" Emily asked.

"He is not my friend. Just a silly boy in my class." Winnie's face got hot.

Annie said, "Don't be embarrassed, Winnie. It's not Connor that Emily is interested in, 'tis his brother, Owen." With a teasing grin, she elbowed Emily's side.

"Doesn't matter much how I feel about Owen now, does it? I'll be on a ship bound for America next week," Emily said. Her lower lip quivered, and Winnie wondered just how much Emily liked this boy.

"Well, there are plenty of rich men in America for you, Emily!" Annie laughed shrilly. "Besides, Sarah Sludden will take very good care of Owen, I've no doubt." Annie poked Emily's side, and ran off ahead.

"Has she gone mad?" Winnie asked.

"Oh, she's just nervous about the trip." Emily stuffed tight fists into her pinafore pockets.

They continued walking in uncomfortable silence until Annie called from up ahead. "Come on! Let's have a look at that grand apple tree in the orchard." She pointed to a tree up a small hill in a farmer's orchard.

"No. Annie, you know as well as I that Da has a perfectly good store of apples for the taking," said Emily.

"Ah, yes, but they taste so much better when they are stolen from a farmer's orchard," said Annie. Batting her eyelashes, she pleaded, "Please?"

Emily's posture relaxed. "Well, I suppose one apple each won't be missed." In years past, the girls had often indulged in an apple or pear on their way home from school.

Annie took off like a skittish rabbit, her white pinafore flapping in the breeze as she aimed for the tallest tree in the meadow.

Emily reached for Winnie's hand and they walked to the tree at a slower pace, curiously watching Annie's frenzied behavior.

"She's absolutely daft," Winnie said to Emily.

"Perhaps . . ." Emily hesitated. They watched as Annie pulled her lanky legs up the tree, branch by branch, until she was right over their heads.

"Careful, Annie, there's some rain in the air. Branches might be a bit slippery." Emily's face tightened.

"Oh, come on now, have a little fun! Come and join me! The apples are lovely, and the best ones are way up here." Annie complexion was unusually flushed, and her dark eyes flashed.

"Why don't you throw us down a good one?" asked Winnie.

"All right, then, suit yourself . . . Here you go." Annie stretched out far to grab a plump red apple at the tip of a slender branch.

"Annie, be careful . . ." started Emily. She stopped in horror, clasping her hands to her chest. Annie had lost her footing. Her worn black leather shoes had no traction on the slick branch. Annie careened through the tree limbs, landing squarely at Winnie and Emily's feet with a stunned look on her face.

"Oomph!" The air escaped from Annie's chest.

Winnie screamed.

Emily draped herself over Annie's fallen body. "Say something, Annie . . . are you all right? Are you hurt?" Tears sprung from Emily's blue eyes, and she joined Winnie in her sobs.

Suddenly, catching her breath, Annie focused her eyes on Emily and gasped, "I've just lost my breath, now, I think I'm all right." She pushed her hands against the ground and tried to sit up. "Ow! My leg, my leg . . . it hurts so much. I can't bear it!" Annie's face went white and she fell back down, unconscious.

"Winnie, fetch Da, please go fast. I'll stay here with Annie. Go now!" Emily waved her hands, frantically motioning for Winnie to run off.

Winnie sucked in a breath and ran. She raced faster than she had ever run before, faster than she had run to chase Connor. She had to find Da. Down the lane she ran and ran. With relief, she spotted him in a pasture, tending a calf. "Da! Da! There's been a terrible accident!" Winnie shouted cross a knoll, nearly colliding into Da.

"Hold on, now, Rosebud, slow down and tell me what happened," Da said, his knuckles whitening as he gripped the calf's rope tighter.

"It's Annie. She's been hurt. She fell out of the apple tree and she looks like a ghost, and now she's unconscious, and Em is standing guard, and oh, please Da, go and make her better!"

Da dropped the calf's rope and pivoted towards the lane. "Take me to her!"

With Winnie leading the way, they ran together without speaking, but not in silence. Her eardrums pounded like thunder. The lane seemed endless, but neither Winnie nor Da would allow themselves to stop.

"Come quick, Da, Annie's over here!" Emily beckoned from the orchard, leaning over her sister's limp body.

"Oh, darling Annie." Da said, worry etched into the lines of his face.

"She said her leg hurt before she passed out. Look at her leg. Doesn't look right." Emily pointed to Annie's shin. Da pursed his lips in sympathetic pain and nodded.

"Well, looks like it might be a break. We'll have Emily go fetch Doctor Fulton. Tell him it's an emergency. We need him to come to the house right away," Da said.

Emily gathered up her long skirt and hurried down the lane, as Da tenderly gathered Annie up into his strong arms. Annie's eye's blinked open. "Da, it hurts more than I can bear," she moaned.

"There now, dear Annie. Da will get you home where we can warm you up. Winnie, you come along as well. We'll surely need your help."

Winnie nodded obediently. But a tiny voice nagged at her. Had Annie fallen on purpose? What would become of Annie's trip to America? Winnie tossed these thoughts aside. How foolish to be thinking such things when there was an emergency at hand. But still, the thought would not stay buried, and continued to rise and haunt her.

Chapter 7
Why Should My Heart Be Sad?

"It's a broken bone, all right. A clean break right above the ankle," Doctor Fulton said, meeting Da's eyes. "I've made a plaster cast and later, you can fashion some crutches from a tree branch. There'll be no activity for this young lady for several weeks. Bones need time to mend."

Winnie leaned against Emily in the corner of the room watching Doctor Fulton. Annie lay in a cot beside the hearth. Across the room at the threshold, Ma braced herself against the doorjamb, Tommy huddled in the folds of her skirt.

"Well, I suppose Annie won't be well enough to make her trip next week," Da said. He rubbed his furrowed brow with his hand waiting for Doctor Fulton's answer.

"Most certainly not. Annie will need to rest quietly for a fortnight, and I will come by to check her progress. She's young and healthy, thank God, and should heal quite nicely. However, a journey is out of the question." Doctor Fulton began to pack up his physician's bag. "I've got another patient to tend to. Mrs. Everett is in labor and having a bad time of it." He headed for the front door.

Ma and Da followed him. "Thank you so very much, Doctor."

Winnie could hear Da's voice outside explaining to Doctor Fulton that he would pay him as soon as he had sold one of the calves. Winnie knew the family couldn't spare to sell it. She sat down somberly at the bench.

Annie was only half awake. The effect of Doctor Fulton's ether medicine had not worn off yet. Her blank eyes were partly covered by heavy lids, and her dry lips were slightly open. She looked like a porcelain doll, her features pale and motionless.

Ma beckoned to Emily and whispered something in her ear. Emily led Tommy out of the room.

Ma knelt beside Annie and kissed her forehead. She left some flour on Annie's face, as she had been kneading bread dough before Annie's accident. Her apron had snowy white flour sprayed upon it and her hair was whitened by some flyaway powder. Her brown eyes looked as though they'd sunken deeper into her face as she stood and motioned to Da.

With a deep sigh, Da pulled himself up from his stool beside Annie's cot. He locked into Ma's gaze. They moved to the edge of the room and spoke in hushed tones. Winnie could not hear what they were saying, but the atmosphere felt as heavy as a funeral.

At one point, both of her parents looked at her in unison. When Winnie glanced up questioningly, they quickly looked away, resuming their whispers. Finally, Ma rested her thin hand on Da's waist and they embraced. Ma turned her head and her brown eyes washed over Winnie. What were they discussing? Winnie's heart pumped wildly.

Ma heaved a weary sigh, dropped her gaze to the floor and as she left the room, brushed a feather-light hand across Winnie's arm.

Winnie whipped her head towards Da. He cradled his face in his hands for a moment, then looked directly at her.

"Da?" Winnie's voice caught, as if it were snagged on a thorn.

"Rosebud . . . there's something we need to discuss . . ." Da paused to take a deep breath, a grimace spreading across his face.

"What? . . . Are you saying . . . If Annie can't go, then I have to go?"

Da nodded yes, his blue eyes dulled by a mist of tears.

"No, I won't go, I can't go, it's not fair!" Winnie charged out of the house, propelled by indignation and sheer terror.

She tore out of the house and down the lane, frizzy hair whipping at her face. She ran and ran until it hurt to breathe. Her body moved by its own accord, her mind a fierce incoherent blackness. Her legs steered her to a familiar spot. The grass was still pressed down in the rectangular shape of a quilt from summer picnics.

Winnie collapsed into a sobbing heap and buried her face in the crook of her elbow. She sank into the nothingness of despair.

Chapter 8
The Rustling Grass

After what seemed an eternity of crying, Winnie's forearms began to itch against the grass, and she shivered as gray clouds covered the setting sun. She sat up and hugged herself to get warm. If she could just take stock of the situation logically, perhaps she'd find a way to manage. She pulled in a quivering breath. "Annie's broken her leg, and she can't go to America, so now I will go in her place." The sound of her own voice stating the facts still did not make her believe. How could she possibly continue to live without Ma and Da?

"Winnie! Winnie!" Emily's familiar voice floated down the lane.

Winnie peered over the tall grass, her face twisted, torn between wanting to be rescued and wanting to run away. She eeked out a squeaky, "Emily?"

"Oh, Winnie!" Emily rushed to Winnie's hideout and, with a relieved sigh, sat beside her. "I'm so glad you're all right."

"Well, I'm not all right. I'll never be all right." Winnie folded her arms and pouted.

"Winnie, I won't try to talk you out of feeling bad. Of course you are upset. I'll just tell you one thing. I'll stay by your side and get you through this the best I can. We'll always have each other." Emily's pretty face peered into Winnie's distraught eyes and the two girls fell into a hug.

"There, there . . . 'twill be all right," Emily said, drawing Winnie up to her feet. "And there's another reason I came to fetch you. All the chickens have gotten out of the pen and I've managed to get all of them but Clucky. I'm just not fast enough to catch her," Emily said, pulling Winnie towards the sloped pasture behind their farmhouse.

Winnie felt skeptical. Was Emily tricking her so that she'd agree to go home?

"Look up there. See that flash of feathers in the briars? Clucky is so stubborn, she won't let me near her." Emily pointed, and in the dim light of the late afternoon, Winnie could just make out the hen. "Please, Winnie. Ma and Da can't spare to lose our best hen."

Winnie drew in a deep breath. "All right, I'll try." She half-heartedly jogged up the slope calling, "Clucky, Clucky, tch, tch, tch." The hen froze and stared at her with black bean eyes. Winnie eased closer and gently lifted the bird. "There you go, Clucky, now you'll be safe from the foxes." Winnie carried her to the henhouse. Fastening the door tightly, she looked over to Emily who was smiling mysteriously. "Why are you grinning at me like that?"

"Well, since Da just mowed the pasture this afternoon, I thought it must be time for a roll down the hill."

Winnie inhaled. A strong scent of freshly cut grass tickled her nose. But didn't Emily understand how terrified Winnie felt? Certainly she should know that even though she loved this game, she was in no mood to play now. "I don't want to roll down the hill now."

"Well, you'll just have to catch me. I daresay you can't outrun your big sister," Emily called, plodding up the hill slowly, weighed down by her heavy woolen skirt.

Winnie's strained face eased into a slight grin. She just couldn't resist the challenge. "You run as slow as a turtle, Em!" The weight of her dark mood dropped away like a discarded cloak as she ran at breakneck speed to the summit and cried out, "Beat you!" Breathing hard, she plopped onto the short grass, wound up her arms tightly across her chest and did side spins down the hill. For several seconds, with increasing momentum, she tumbled downward out of control. It dawned on Winnie that this was just like her fate. Gravity will just take over, she thought; it was out of her control. An alternating view of sky, earth, sky, earth, dizzied her until she could no longer tell top from bottom. Was it good or bad to go to America? She didn't know . . . she was just so dizzy! "Just let gravity take me along," she whispered to herself.

Emily was soon to follow, abandoning her newfound maturity of sixteen years to the wind.

The girls scurried back up to the peak several more times until at last, exhausted, they lay on the grass at the bottom, and looked upward at the darkening sky.

"'Tis teatime, and Ma and Da will surely be worried." Emily coaxed Winnie up from the grass and the two sisters approached the small house.

Walking up the path, it occurred to Winnie for the first time in her two years of living at the farm, that her family was poor. The tin roof was rusted and patched. The glass pane window was cracked with no hope of repair for lack of money. Da had been fortunate to have been given this property, long abandoned when a farmer's widow had died. Surely the Weirs had made improvements by the sweat of their labors, but when it came to replacing items that required buying, they fell short. No matter how hard they worked, there never was enough food or money. Maybe Da was right about going to America.

Emily and Winnie entered the house, which was dimly illuminated by a few oil lamps. Ma, Da, and Tommy looked up expectantly from the table as they came in. Annie lay asleep in the corner.

"Emmie, Winnie!" Tommy's chapped red cheeks broke into a smile and he clapped his hands.

"Come, now, girls. Come have some tea. We were so worried, with the sun going down." Da went to the scullery and returned with some scones and tea. It was rare that Da did the kitchen work, but today was a very different day.

"Is that a slight tinge of green I detect about the knees of your stockings?" he asked, grinning as he poured the tea.

Emily and Winnie answered sheepishly, "Yes, Da, we were rolling down the hill."

"Well, there certainly are some things that must be tended to. Rolling down a freshly mowed hill of grass, for one thing. Someone's got to take care of that!" Da chuckled and poured some tea into Winnie's cup.

Sleepiness descended upon Winnie like a leaden veil as she settled into her spot on the family bench. This had been a very long day. She barely had the strength to lift her teacup.

Annie continued to doze as Ma and Da picked at the food. Winnie nibbled at half a scone and took a sleepy sip from her tea cup. Tommy did his usual banging and splattering until Emily settled him down for the night. Ma slipped away into her room, leaving Winnie and Da to tidy up the table.

"Leave the ware. I'll take care of it later," Da said to Winnie. "Let's sit by the hearth and I'll tell a story."

Winnie didn't argue, and when Emily came back, she joined them at the hearth. Annie's sleeping silhouette was a constant reminder to Winnie of her new future. Winnie rested her weight against Da, closed her eyes and let his voice lull her into a sleepy haze. He was telling a tale of Little Rosie and the brownie known as Tod Lowrie.

> *No one had ever actually seen a brownie before. Tod Lowrie, the brownie, recognized a brave soul when he saw one, and so, that night, he came to do Little Rosie's many labors. Rosie woke from her sleep to hear a rustling in the kitchen. When she peered around the cupboard, there he was: little red cap, pointy ears, green shoes. And he had done all her chores! The hearth swept so clean it shined like crystal, the soda bread baked, the stockings mended, the linen ironed. With a huge sneeze, up the chimney he went. It is said that only those with a pure and brave heart will be rewarded by the sight of a brownie, and Little Rosie was just that person.*

Winnie was remotely aware of being transported to her bed by strong arms. Kissed tenderly and tucked in, she settled into fairy dreams.

Chapter 9
O Let Me Ne'er Forget

Upon awakening the next morning, Winnie wasn't sure if it had all been a dream. It was nearly dawn, and since she was the first to rise, she crept in stocking feet to the front room and saw Ma sleeping in a chair beside Annie's cot. Ma was still wearing her clothes from yesterday. One of her hands rested lightly upon Annie's blanket. Beneath the blanket, Annie's cast made a high ridge.

So it was real. Winnie was going to America in less than a week.

Her stomach flipped as she considered this turn of events. There was so little time to prepare. Annie had had months to get ready. She swallowed back her fear, knowing she'd need to continue on with daily life, chores included. What else could she do? No matter how dizzy she felt, she'd let gravity take over.

Tiptoeing back to her bedroom, she dressed silently, trying not to awaken Emily. Beautiful, grown-up Emily.

Winnie walked to the outhouse by the dim light of the autumn dawn. The days were getting shorter, and soon she'd be doing her chores in the dark. No, her chores would be done by someone else. She'd be in Stamford, America, doing American chores for an American aunt.

She aimed towards the henhouse. Dear Clucky. Would Aunt Mabel have a henhouse for her to tend? Winnie collected a small pile of brown eggs and set them down in a basket beside the scullery door. She picked up an empty bucket by its cool metal handle and remembered how she'd heard that in America they had taps with running water indoors. No more early morning traipses to the well.

When Winnie returned to the house, Ma was bent over Annie. They were talking quietly with faces mirroring strong emotions. Winnie felt a sharp sting of jealousy.

Ma looked up. "Winnie." She beckoned her to come closer.

Feeling uneasy, Winnie asked, "What is it Ma? Are you well?"

"I am well enough. It's Annie that's not well today." Ma reached out for Annie's limp hand, and again Winnie felt a piercing stab of jealousy. "I was just explaining to Annie how she'd need to stay home to mend her bone," Ma continued. "I told her how you'll be going to America instead."

Winnie's eyes darted to check Annie's face for a reaction, but Annie continued to stare vacantly into the flames of the fire.

"You'll not be going to school anymore, Winnie. Emily will tell Miss Whivisty. And you'll need to pack for your journey." Ma removed her hand from Annie, and rested it on Winnie's shoulder.

Winnie's eyes welled up. Ma's touch had sent a jolt of self-pity through her body. How she longed for Ma to tell her she could stay home too.

"Winnie, you are a Weir. Do this for your family." For the first time in months, Ma gazed at her with clarity, conviction, and, Winnie thought, affection. "Emily will take good care of you."

Winnie's voice quivered as she said, "Yes, Ma."

Ma's eyes drifted away and the spell was broken. "I slept so poorly in this chair last night. I need to lie down now."

Through a film of tears, Winnie watched Ma shuffle to her bedroom.

Tommy came trotting out to the hearth, dragging an old baby quilt. He sucked on one corner that had turned brown from this two-year-long habit.

"Annie has a bad leg." Tommy pointed to the ungainly white cast with a look of deep concern.

Emily, who had stepped across through the doorway from the scullery to set out the ware, said, "Yes, Tommy, she broke her leg. But it will get better. Go give her a kiss." Emily and Winnie watched as Tommy bent down and kissed the cold white plaster.

"Not that thing! Kiss her cheek!" Emily laughed, and Annie couldn't help but grin. Winnie felt a smile creep across her face. The tension of the last twenty-four hours eased.

Da entered the house with a bucket of milk. "Now that's music to my ears! The lovely sound of Weir women laughing." Tommy joined in with exaggerated laughter, and Da said, "And Weir men, too!" Da gave Winnie a hug with his strong arms, and she lingered in his embrace an extra moment.

Settling into their places at the table, Da said, "Let's have a blessing." Emily helped Tommy put his little hands together. "Dear Father in heaven, bless this food we are about to eat and guide us in our daily work. Bless William in heaven beside you, bless Ma and her unborn child, bless wee Tommy. Give Annie the strength to heal and lead our dear Emily and Winifred safely across the ocean to a land of plenty. Amen."

Winnie looked over at Emily to see her reaction to Da's mentioning of the journey to America.

Emily smiled back. "Would you care for some strawberry jam, Winnie?"

"Of course!" Winnie was beginning to feel as if she belonged to a special club. She was about to embark upon a journey that was acceptable to Emily, so it would be acceptable to her as well. Winnie would be forced to give up her life at the farm, wee Tommy, Annie, Ma, and Da, and in return, she'd get opportunity, America, and Emily. Maybe she could manage with Emily by her side, her one consolation. And maybe it wouldn't be too long before the rest of the family would join them.

Although Winnie tried to make each moment last an eternity, the few remaining days at Corbally were a blur of cleaning, mending, and packing. Da was preoccupied with tending a calf that had died despite his best efforts. Ma pieced together fabric from her own best skirt to sew a new pinafore for Winnie.

Two days before the girl's departure, Da planned a trip to town. Fintona was the biggest town nearby, and at three miles away, he and Winnie could walk down the lane with some goods and the remaining calf to sell at the market. Emily would need to stay home and tend Tommy and Annie while Ma rested. Winnie made a bundle of jars of butter, a sack of potatoes, and some spare vegetables from the farm.

Emily joined Winnie in the scullery. "Winnie, here's some lace

I've been working on. Ma says Mrs. Mulhern might be interested in buying it." Mrs. Mulhern was an old friend of Ma's who owned a dressmaker's shop in town. "And here, Ma wants you to deliver this note to Mrs. Mulhern as well." Emily handed an envelope with Ma's graceful script across the top: "Anna Mulhern." Ma was a letter writer. While she remained distant in the everyday chores of the household, she continued her teacher-like habit of writing. Winnie was more than a little curious about what Ma had written, but she dare not appear too nosy. She tucked the sealed envelope into a sack and filled a pail with a picnic for two.

"Let's head out now," Da said, lifting the heaviest sack across his shoulder, pulling a calf by a rope with his other hand. Winnie trotted behind him, pail in hand.

Coming over the hill from behind the farm, Winnie spotted Emily's best friend. "Emily, Sara's coming!" Winnie called. She was glad for Emily to have the company of her friend. Whenever the two girls got together, there was lots of giggling and fussing about boys. Winnie didn't quite understand their fascination, especially Sara's apparent interest in Owen Quinn. Winnie suspected that Owen fancied Emily. But boys were of little use to Winnie. They only seemed interested in getting dirty and pulling braids.

"Be sure to stop in at the drapery store and see the latest style of shoes, Winnie," Emily said. Although they would not be buying anything, it was always fun to look.

"Oh, yes!" said Winnie, feeling proud that she was able to help her big sister.

With a cheery sky overhead, Da and Winnie set out. Da was excited to tell her all about the wonders of America. "In America, they've got huge houses, with wooden floors and a second story. Some even have three stories! In the scullery, they call it the kitchen, there are ice boxes to keep the food fresh over time. There's water in pipes that lead into the house and come out of a tap, Rosebud! Can you imagine? No outhouses. Instead, they've got a privy inside the house that flushes away the waste."

"What kind of house does Aunt Mabel have, Da?"

"I'm not sure, but it must be as big as a palace. She's got boarders. That's where you and Emily help out. You girls will be showing off your British hospitality for her American boarders.

But I'll tell you one more thing: Aunt Mabel runs several markets, so you will be cooking the most splendid foods you can imagine. The finest cuts of beef, lamb, duck!"

Winnie's mouth watered, imagining her life as a princess in America. But then she remembered the part about working to keep the boarders happy. "Do you think there'll be time to play, Da?"

"Of course, Rosebud. Lots of Weir cousins to meet. But, as Ma and I have always taught you, a girl gets ahead in life through hard work, education, and faith in the good Lord."

Winnie nodded, a little uneasy with the notion of working so hard for unknown American boarders. She had one last question, "Da, how long will it be before you come to America with Tommy, Ma, Annie, and the baby?"

Da paused and said, "Let's sit down for a rest and have our picnic." Da tied the calf to a tree and patted a spot on a thick log that had fallen on the side of the lane. Winnie sidled close and handed Da some brown bread.

"Well, there are some things, my dear Rosebud, that only time will tell. 'Twill be over a year at least, what with the broken leg, a new baby, and no money." Da bit into the bread and chewed thoughtfully. "You must put your trust in God."

Winnie sipped from a bottle of milk and wiped her mouth with her sleeve. "Yes, Da."

"Remember, you must be grateful to your aunt for this opportunity she has provided. Having you stay with her and paying for your fare, and all the rest." Da reached into the sack and pulled out an apple. "The steamship ride will be quite an adventure, with all of the latest inventions. Why, the advertisements said the ship was built in Glasgow, Scotland, just last year. There'll be electric lights, food served in a dining room, and a special dormitory for you and Emily to sleep in, just for unmarried women. And don't forget Lizzie Askin. Remember that nice lady we met in church? She will be there to help you out."

Da seemed very excited about the plan, so Winnie smiled. They continued down the lane, and Da chatted about what he'd heard about life in America. Images of rich Americans in stylish clothing and fantastical inventions danced in Winnie's mind.

The smell of coal burning signaled that they had arrived in

Fintona. Da steered Winnie down the main street to the market so that they could unload their goods to sell. Da also liked to catch up with old friends and fellow farmers, finding out the latest news.

"Now remember, Winnie, when you pass someone on the street, it is important to greet them with a 'hello' and a smile." Of course, on the country lanes of Corbally, it was easy to greet the rare passer-by, but in the busier streets of Fintona, it took a little more work. Winnie looked up and smiled her "hellos" as several shoppers passed by.

Once inside the market, Da negotiated with a merchant. Winnie had a quick look around. Standing upon a concrete floor with a fine layer of sawdust upon it, she looked across the vast indoor warehouse to the other end. There were live animals milling about, their owners expounding upon the virtues of the breed. Winnie didn't know who was louder, the animals or the humans. There were merchants selling baskets of potatoes, turnips, cabbage, and brussels sprouts. Nothing she couldn't get fresh at her farm, and anyway, she was quite bored by her family's steady diet of these vegetables. Shelves of baked goods, dairy products, and preserves tempted her. She eyed the strawberry jam, but knew that although they were nearly done with the family's supply of preserves from the spring, they did not have the money for such a luxury item.

"Rosebud, why don't you go along to see Mrs. Mulhern?" Da said. "I've got some more fellows to see here and Ma would like you to deliver her letter."

"Yes, Da." Winnie was glad to move along, and ready to take in more sights along the main street. "I'll meet you back here."

She strolled down the street and stopped to look in the window of the drapery store. Bolts of the finest Irish linen and ornate bonnets decorated with plumes from exotic birds filled the window front. There were shoes of every size and shape, some high, some low, all made of shiny new leather. She memorized the design of the latest shoe style so that she could describe it to Emily later.

When Winnie entered the dress shop, a young lady she did not know stood at the counter. "May I help you?" she asked.

"Yes, Ma'am, I've come to see Mrs. Mulhern. My ma has a letter for her."

The lady smiled kindly and replied, "Have a seat, lass, and I'll go fetch her. It may take a few minutes, so please make yourself comfortable. There's a catalogue you might like to look at." She pointed to an enormous volume titled, *Sears and Roebuck Catalogue.*

"Thank you, Ma'am." Winnie eagerly took the tome into her lap and began to turn the pages. There were advertisements for items for which she had never sensed a need. There were organs for making music, seemingly an essential for every American parlor, a talking machine called a "Victrola" that made music when cranked by a handle. Who would need an ice box, thought Winnie, if the cow was right outside your scullery door? Hanging from Mrs. Mulhern's shelves was a newspaper cutting showing the most amazing thing Winnie could imagine: a flying machine! Sure, she had heard about Henry Ford's Model-T. A true marvel that a cart could move without a horse. But what was this about flying? The idea seemed so magical. Winnie edged closer and squinted to read the fine print. "Wilbur Wright Circles the Statue of Liberty." Winnie wondered what it would feel like to soar with the birds in the sky. The machine looked so flimsy, but the caption clearly stated that this American man had flown above a river in New York and as high as that tremendous statue.

Mrs. Mulhern, a stylishly dressed matron, entered the front room. "Well, hello, Winifred! My how you've grown. And how much you take after your father. I'd never take you for Isabella's daughter . . ." Winnie wondered if this was a compliment or not, and brushed her hand self-consciously over her front teeth.

"Hello, Mrs. Mulhern," she rose to greet the dressmaker.

"What brings you to Fintona? Is your mother well?" Mrs. Mulhern asked.

"Oh, we are all well. Ma is very tired, due to the baby coming this winter, but she sends her regards. She gave me this letter to give to you." As Winnie pulled the letter out, Emily's lace fell out.

"Gracious, look at this beautiful lace! Is this your mother's work?" Mrs. Mulhern took the letter as Winnie bent down to pick up the fallen lace.

"Oh, no, Mrs. Mulhern, 'tis Emily's work. We were wondering if you'd be interested in buying it for dressmaking." Winnie suddenly felt a little shy.

"Absolutely! This is quite fine. Your mother certainly has done a brilliant job teaching Emily!" Mrs. Mulhern took the lace into her hands and inspected it. She went to a cash register and pulled out some coins.

"Now then, here is a little something for the lace. I apologize that it isn't more, but as you know, money is scarce."

Winnie had never held so many metal coins in her palm at once. "Thank you very much for your kindness, Mrs. Mulhern." She head for the door.

Mrs. Mulhern said, "And be sure to tell your ma that I'm praying for her health."

"Yes, Mrs. Mulhern." Winnie trotted off down the street, finding Da waiting for her at the market.

"There's my Rosebud. I've got a few coins here in my pocket. Maybe we can stop in the butcher shop and buy some duckling for our last supper together in Corbally before your journey."

"I've got some more coins to add to our fortune," Winnie said, displaying the money Emily's lace had earned.

"Well, then, Winnie, we'd best be off. 'Tis a long walk home and we've no lantern for the dark. Just a quick stop at the butcher shop."

Da steered Winnie into the shop, a place the Weirs rarely visited, since they ate meat sparingly, and when they did, it was slaughtered cattle or chicken from their own farm. Winnie did not care for the smell of the shop and was relieved to head out the door, a small sack of duckling slung over her shoulder.

The walk home passed rather quickly, with Da relaying the news of town to Winnie. Lizzie Askin's Da had been at the market, excited to discuss his daughter's plans to go to Brooklyn, New York. Many others had grown children heading to America shortly.

As Da and Winnie approached their house, they saw Emily and Sara chasing after Tommy in the front yard.

"Hello, Da, Winnie!" Emily ran down the slope to greet them. "Sara says that her family will be hosting a crossroads dance tomorrow! May I go?" Her face radiated excitement.

"Of course you may." Da plodded up the front path, weary from a long day of walking. Tommy scooted closer to hug his ankles. "And how was my wee Tommy today?" Da bent down and lifted Tommy high.

"Tommy was a good boy." Tommy smiled proudly.

"Yes, I'm sure, and how is your ma and poor Annie?" Da peered into the dark front room.

"Da," came Annie's weak voice from the cot.

Ma was dozing beside Annie's cot. Her eyes opened abruptly as Da entered the cottage.

"Da, I'm fine, but I am nearly going out of my mind with boredom!" Annie propped herself up on elbows.

"Ah, yes, dear Annie. Patience, time will heal." Da approached her cot and stooped down to kiss Ma. "And my Isabella. How are you faring today?"

Ma cleared the sleep from her throat and said, "Just fine at the moment, all things considered."

"I'll go fetch us all some tea. Tea and a little gossip from town will certainly help!"

While Da chatted, Winnie went outside to watch Emily and Sara. Sixteen-year-old girls were quite entertaining.

"I'll wear my new dress, the one with the red print across the neck and shoulders," Sara was telling Emily.

"Yes, I know that dress. Red, the better to catch Owen Quinn's eye!" Emily teased as Sara's face reddened.

"I thought he fancied you, Emily," Sara said.

"Well, we'll just have to find out tomorrow night." Emily giggled. She looked over at Winnie who was staring, mouth agape.

"How about joining us at the crossroads, Winnie? Da and Ma might let you come too," Emily said.

"I'd love to!" Without a moment's hesitation, Winnie scrambled to the door to ask for permission. But before she was through the doorway, Emily called behind her, "And I am sure that Connor will be there as well!"

"Ugh!" Winnie groaned.

Chapter 10
Round Me Rings the Music of the Spheres
A Crossroads Dance

Not only did Ma and Da give Winnie permission to attend the crossroads dance, the whole family decided to come along. It would be the perfect way to see the girls off before their journey, Da had said. Even Annie could hobble along on her new crutches, whittled by Da from the branch of an apple tree. If it was an apple tree that got the bone broken, then it would be an apple tree that got the bone mended, he had said.

Emily had stayed up late the night before to add an edge of embroidery upon the borders of the family's old linens. After mending, scrubbing, and ironing the cloth, they sparkled like the finest from the drapery shop of Fintona.

At half past noon, the family sat down to dine on duckling stew. The table was set with the best ware and linen.

After eating his share, Da surveyed the humble table and said, "A meal fit for a king!" He wiped his mouth with the edge of a restored napkin. "Looks like you've enjoyed the meal as well, Tommy."

Everyone looked over at Tommy who wore duckling gravy on his chin like a beard. "Yummy! More!" Tommy watched eagerly as Emily pushed some of her portion onto his plate.

Even Ma seemed to have enjoyed the meal. "It was very good," she said. "Emily, why don't you head up to the Sluddens now to help with the preparations? And bring some buttermilk for the soda bread."

"Oh, yes, Ma. Winnie, you can finish tidying up." Emily bent over to kiss Ma's cheek and dashed out the scullery door.

"I've got to finish up some field work, and before sundown, we can leave for the crossroads," Da said. He excused himself from the table and went to the back door to get his cap to head for the pasture.

As soon as the ware was washed and dried, Winnie helped Annie get dressed. The two girls wore matching pinafores with pretty lace collars crocheted by Emily. This afternoon Winnie was happy to smooth down her thick brown hair and capture it into two neat braids. She also brushed out Annie's hair, and when Ma called out for a hand with Tommy, Winnie was more than willing. With a party ahead, her mood was excited, full of nervous energy. She also felt special, since the dance tonight was planned in honor of Emily's and her departure tomorrow.

"Tommy, let's go out back and I'll teach you how to play hopscotch." Winnie missed Annie's outdoor companionship, and she was desperate to have anyone play with her, even if it was her two-year-old brother.

"First, you find a stone just the right size." Winnie and Tommy searched the ground for a pebble, until Tommy settled on a stone nearly the size of a boulder embedded deep within the earth. "No, Tommy, that one is far too big. A stone just about this size." Winnie held up her lucky pebble, and Tommy nodded. He grabbed at the first pebble he spied on the ground. It was barely bigger than the nail of his pinkie. "Now that one is too small!"

Hopscotch with Tommy would be impossible.

Da walked up the path from a few hours' labor in the fields. Exhausted and dirty, he wiped sweat from his forehead. But, he looked very happy to see Winnie and Tommy. "Well, if it isn't my two dance partners! Are you ready for the crossroads dance?"

"Yes, Da, but you need to wash up." Winnie shoulders slumped. She was beginning to feel a little impatient and worried that she'd miss the fun.

"Well, Rosebud, I'll hurry for you. But only if you promise me the first dance." Da paused to catch his breath.

"Of course!" Winnie could not stand still. She started hopping on the hopscotch grid, with Tommy following a little too closely behind.

Finally, a half hour later, Da led Ma and Annie out of the house. Annie managed quite well on her crutches. "Ma, remember that lullaby you used to sing when I was wee? Could we sing it all together?" Annie asked.

Ma smiled and shook her head, "I don't know if I can remember it."

Da said, "Oh, come now, we'll all sing it together. 'Tis the Last Rose of Summer." Da started and everyone joined in, singing as they walked, adjusting their pace to Annie's rhythm on crutches. The sun was close to the horizon, promising a colorful sunset for the festivities.

A crowd of neighbors had gathered at the crossroads, and a couple of men wearing tweed caps tuned their fiddles. Another old farmer had an accordion. The musicians sat down upon their stools and conferred about the music.

Emily came running down to see her family, looking radiant. "Ma! Da! Annie! Would you like to come inside and have some tea with Mr. and Mrs. Sludden?"

"That sounds lovely, Emily. My feet ache," Ma said, pausing to catch her breath.

"I'd love to join you, Isabella, but first I need to have a dance with my Rosebud," Da said.

Ma and Annie went up to the Sludden house. Da took Winnie by the hand, pulling her to the area cleared for dancing. The music was gay and the rhythm quick, making the two jig at quite a lively tempo. The sun had gone down, leaving the dancers to revel in the warm glow of a harvest moon.

When the song ended, Dad said, "Rosebud, my old legs just can't keep up the likes of you. Keep your eye on Tommy, while I go up to the house to join Ma and Annie." Da strode up to the Sludden cottage, its front door wide open, glowing with candlelight within.

Winnie found Tommy, who was stirring up a dark puddle with a short stick. She watched for the right moment to break into the game of tag that had just started in the field. Tommy attempted to play, running as fast as his short legs could manage, making a sound like a whinnying stallion. The younger children yelled and screamed in delighted voices for the next few hours, the older children danced, and the adults sat on stools, singing, sipping tea, and chatting.

Hannah Curran was among the children, and she, Tommy, and Winnie were a team at a game which combined tag with hide and seek. Under the cover of dark, they ducked from bush to bush, as the opposing team sought to capture them. Once tagged and captured, they would be thrown into a jail, made up of an enclosure of thorny shrubs. Tommy was imprisoned several times, but Winnie made sure to rescue him each time.

Finally, at about ten o'clock, Da said, "All good things must come to an end, I'm afraid." He scooped up a sleeping Tommy from a hideout he and Winnie had made behind some tall grass. "But before we go, I must have one last dance."

Ma and Annie watched dreamily as Da held wee Tommy, and waltzed to the tune of "I'll Take You Home again, Kathleen." Da reached out for Ma and the three danced together for the last verse.

Winnie sat on a stone wall beside the other farm children, feeling the ping of tired leg muscles unwinding. She glanced sideways at Connor Quinn, who had kept his distance, for fear of being beaten in tag once again. His knickers had torn at the knee after he'd tripped on the roots of a beech tree. His freckled face was bright red and sweaty. Winnie wondered whatever did Emily and Sara see in boys?

Emily's cheeks were flushed from a night of dancing with just about every boy in Corbally. It was as if she were a member of royalty, and everyone wanted a moment with her to say goodbye. Owen Quinn had followed her around like a puppy until finally he managed to get one dance with her. After that, he'd spent the rest of the night dancing with Sara Sludden, but Winnie noticed him slipping in glances at Emily every now and then.

The Weir family gathered to leave as neighbors shook hands, with special farewells to Emily and Winnie. Winnie thought that if Emily was royalty, then she must be a younger princess, or at least a lady-in-waiting.

Da tucked in his three daughters, their last night to sleep in that old bed together. Feigning sleep, Winnie heard the soft shuffle of her mother's stocking feet approaching her room. She watched Ma bend down to unlatch the bags she and Emily had packed. Ma slid an envelope within each of their bags.

Winnie said, "Ma?"

"There, now, Winnie, you need your sleep for tomorrow." Ma turned towards the door and stepped through the threshold.

"Ma?" Winnie choked out huskily.

Ma paused at the door and said, "I've left a letter for each of you in your bags. You may read it when you are on the ship."

"Thank you, Ma."

"'Tis a great journey you are about to take. May God bless you, dear child." Ma disappeared into the darkness.

Winnie felt tears gathering and she stifled a sob.

"Winnie, it's all right," came a soft voice from the other side of the bed. It was Emily. Winnie had thought that both she and Annie had been sleeping. Annie continued to snore lightly.

"I just don't know how I'll be able to leave," Winnie wailed, releasing more tears.

Emily rolled over and held Winnie. "Ma and Da love us so much that they want what's best for us. You've got to believe that, Winnie."

"But it's just so hard," Winnie said, using her nightgown sleeve to sop up her tears.

"Yes. Sometimes doing the right thing is the hardest thing to do." Emily smoothed Winnie's hair. "We'll be all right because we'll be together."

Winnie lay back down and wound the edge of the quilt around herself. She would have Emily by her side. And what had Ma written in her letter? She slept lightly that last night, opening her eyes every few hours to see packed bags beside the bed, ready for an early morning walk to the Fintona train station with Da.

Chapter 11
The Mourning Light

Mr. Gargin awoke with the cock's crow at dawn. He filled his black kettle with water and set it on the iron hook above the glowing embers of last night's fire. He added more peat until he had a good blaze, and went to the scullery to cut a slice of soda bread. He wondered if he'd be delivering post in the rain again today, so he paused to have a look at the sky from the front door.

Stepping across the threshold of his thatched roof cottage, he gazed upward and noted the sun struggling to rise behind heavy clouds. Yes, rain again. He'd never get rid of this nagging cough at this rate. He wiped his bulbous nose with a tattered handkerchief and jammed it into the breast pocket of his shirt. Just as he turned to go back inside, something down the lane caught his eye.

In the distance, he spotted the shape of three people carrying bags. Mr. Gargin thought it odd to see anyone going to market this early, so he stayed to watch.

One figure was much taller and moved like a man. The two others were smaller and feminine, even child-like. The smallest figure was tilted at an angle, leaning into the man. Oh dear, 'tis a wee lass and her Da. And another lass. Now who would be traveling?

Mr. Gargin suddenly recalled the gossip from the pub, and he coughed to clear his thickening airways. Now what was it that the fellow had said? 'Twas the Weir family, the farmer from Corbally, John Weir. But only the two girls were going without their Da and Ma. And one having broken her leg. Yes, that was it. The youngest lass had to replace her sister at the last moment.

Mr. Gargin shook his head. This was a sad sight. The trio walked at such a deliberated and rhythmic pace, they must be forcing one leg to follow the other. Mr. Gargin thought of so many others who'd passed this way to the railway on their trips to America. It seemed to him as if it were a funeral march. Might as well have a wake. They'd never be seen again. In the distance, a mourning dove made a plaintive coo. Or was it? Shivering, Mr. Gargin swore he'd heard the wail of a banshee. The Weirs turned a corner, and continued out of view.

Part Two: Of Skies and Seas
At the Landing Stage of Londonderry
October 9, 1909

Chapter 12
Lizzie Askin

Lizzie Askin swiped one last bittersweet tear from her eye as she bade her Da goodbye. She was surprised at how relieved she was to be done with this farewell. Her father guided his horse and carriage through the crowded landing stage of Londonderry harbor and disappeared. She knew she would never see him again. This is his life, now I'll have mine, she thought.

Turning her head towards the harbor, she took in a wondrous sight. In all her thirty years in Fintona, Ireland, she had never encountered a man-made object so large. Before her rose the steamship *California*, built in dimensions she could barely comprehend. *The California* was stationed in the Londonderry Harbor like a long black fortress. Billowy white smoke was drifting from two enormous cylinders. How could this leaden object float, let alone carry its thousand passengers safely across the ocean to America?

Lizzie adjusted her thoughts to a promise she had made. The friendly shopkeeper of Clabby, John Weir, had asked that she keep a watchful eye on his two daughters who were traveling alone to America. John had such high hopes for his family. Unfortunately, like so many others, he did not have the money to take the whole family across the sea to America. It was only the relatives from America who could afford a ticket.

Lizzie brushed her flyaway blonde hair from her face and craned her neck to get a better view of the railroad tracks. A tall and robust woman, she had a good view over the crowd. Sure enough, a train was working its way to the waterfront station.

She hurried through the crowds of fellow British Irish immigrants to get closer to the train platform. Clutching a suitcase in one hand, holding down her new hat with the other, she squeezed past hundreds of people. She couldn't help but hear the desperate last words of goodbye as she passed through the crowd. Crying, hugging, clinging: it was too intimate for Lizzie to watch. While she understood the sadness of goodbye, she also knew the alternative was worse. Life in Ireland for an unmarried woman was like being trapped in a tomb. Lizzie knew if she stayed she was destined to remain an old maid for the rest of her life. No job, no family, aside from the elderly relatives it was assumed she'd nurse through ill health until death, either theirs or hers! No, she was confident in her decision to go to Brooklyn, New York, to work as a servant. Making the decision to go to America was simple. She wanted to live.

The doors of the train opened and passengers with stunned faces stepped out. It seemed as if every one of them needed to pause and absorb the view of the California before descending to the bottom step, luggage in hand.

Lizzie spotted the Weir sisters. First Emily stepped out, her dark blond hair catching the sunlight. She wore her hair like a schoolgirl, two braids tied off with a ribbon. Pretty girl, thought Lizzie. Attached to Emily's hand was a girl, smaller than Lizzie expected. Hadn't John said that Annie, his fourteen-year-old daughter, would be with Emily? But surely, this was the younger girl, Winifred.

Even from a great distance, Lizzie could see from Winnie's cowering posture that she was positively terrified. Poor dear!

Winnie was quite short, perhaps eleven years old, Lizzie guessed.

Her thick brown hair pulled into two braids framed her full-cheeked face. Winnie bore a resemblance to her father, having the same prominent front teeth. A sweet face, thought Lizzie.

"Over here, Emily, Winifred!" Lizzie waved her raised hand and wove through the crowd.

The girls' faces lit with recognition and they hurried across to join her.

"Now then, don't you look lovely dressed in your Sunday best?" Lizzie said. "Wasn't expecting to see Winifred with you, Emily."

"Yes, there's been a bit of a change to the plan. Annie could not make the trip, you see, and so Winnie's taking her place." Emily explained. In spite of her soft measured tones, Winnie broke into sobs at the reminder of her plight.

"What could have happened to Annie?" Lizzie asked.

As Emily explained, Lizzie nodded and noticed that Winnie's entire body was by now heaving with sobs.

"Winnie's having a bit of a bad spell. Understandable, considering the circumstances, Miss Askin," Emily said, running the palm of her hand across her sister's shoulders.

Lizzie gazed at the girls with sympathetic eyes. "First, you must call me Lizzie. And don't be saying you're sorry for having feelings! Just look around and you'll catch an ear-full of feelings." She swept her long arm upwards, indicating a long line of passengers waiting before a ramp. There were hundreds of people on line, most of whom were British Irish. Lizzie looked up to the deck of the California and saw that its rails were brimming with a rainbow of expectant faces. These were the passengers that had already boarded the ship at its first port of Glasgow. There were many fair skinned Scottish faces, but she could also see people dressed in foreign looking clothing. Lizzie guessed that some were from the Scandinavian countries and others appeared to be Russian Jews. There were a few olive skinned passengers, perhaps from Italy. But all of them bore the same hopeful expression as they looked down at the crowd of travelers in Londonderry about to join them on this great journey.

"Would you look at that ship, girls? Have you ever in your life seen anything so large?" Lizzie met the girls' eyes and understood that they needed to take in their situation more slowly. She stopped her chatter and waited in line with the hundreds of others. Lizzie silently vowed that she would see these two sisters safely through the journey. Their fear and sadness tugged at her heartstrings. Nineteen years ago when her own mother had died, she'd been a lonely eleven-year-old girl. Although she was eager to get on with her new life, Lizzie pledged to herself that she would fulfill this promise before she cut her ties with her homeland.

Chapter 13
The Steamship, California
October 14, 1909

Perhaps it was seasickness. Perhaps it was the tepid soup and stringy meat she had barely eaten in the steerage dining hall an hour earlier. In any case, Winnie's stomach was a queasy mixture of dread, excitement, and anticipation as she stood on the deck of the mighty steamship, California. For five days, all she had seen from her favorite bench was a dreary gray stretch of ocean. There was gray everywhere: sky, sea, even the floors of the ship had been painted gray. Winnie noticed how most of the passengers' faces had taken on a gray cast, thanks to the relentless rocking motion of the ship and the resulting seasickness.

She hoped that America would be more colorful than this. She missed the patchwork farm fields and jumble of buildings leaning against each other on the main street of Fintona. She knew so little about Aunt Mable and Stamford, Connecticut. Would Aunt Mabel's house be an "in-town" house, wedged closely among the ships built of stone as she had known in Fintona? Or would her aunt live in a gentleman's country house like Grandda Moffatt's with its acres of pastureland? She knew that Aunt Mable was wealthy, but she wondered what American wealth was like. Lizzie Askin had described the exciting lifestyles of American ladies. She had shared some copies of *The Ladies Home Journal* with Emily and Winnie.

Winnie's memory of Mabel's visit two years ago was so dim. Somehow she couldn't picture Aunt Mabel living the colorful life Lizzie described. Aunt Mabel had seemed, so, well, gray!

Just as waves of bile rose in Winnie's throat from the boat's unsteady motion, homesickness washed up like high tide. She missed Da and Ma fiercely. How she longed for a hug from Ma, a wink and a tale from Da. She took comfort in Emily and even Lizzie, but it was not quite the same. Both Lizzie and Emily were struggling with even worse cases of seasickness. The doctors aboard the California were constantly urging passengers to stay above deck. However, so many had been weakened, barely able to stand. Some passengers had spent the entire five days on their beds, retching into basins.

The stench below was unbearable, so Winnie made every effort to stay on deck. While Emily and Lizzie spent more time resting on their bunks, Winnie preferred the outdoors. Standing before the vast ocean, she thought back to the first days aboard the steamship. When she'd first boarded, she couldn't help but feel awed by the sheer size of the California. It was a floating village! But this was a village of strangers, coming and going, eating, sleeping, in such close quarters . . . It was like nothing she'd ever experienced. Winnie had an especially hard time passing people without saying "hello." There were so many people, it was impossible to acknowledge everyone. Yet Da's voice echoed in her mind: "When you pass someone, it is important to greet them with a 'hello' and a smile."

The ship's crew attempted to make passengers feel at home. The British Irish travelers were grouped together in dormitories, and the dining menu offered the familiar menu of potatoes, boiled vegetables, and meat. Every evening tea was served. Winnie had noticed a different menu for the Russian Jews. Lizzie had explained that it was "kosher" food. Lizzie was an avid reader and had read nearly all the books in the Fintona Branch Library. She had said that kosher was something about Jew's religious practices and the rules about how and what to eat. Winnie thought the kosher food had a pleasant tangy aroma when she passed that dining area.

Lizzie had also told Winnie that the accommodations on the California were luxury compared to a decade ago. Her friend who'd traveled just two years before had not had the modern equipment of this new ship. And Winnie remembered the awful stories Mr. Gargin had told her about the potato famine and immigrants dying on the so-called coffin ships.

The California certainly was a marvel of the latest inventions. With electric power, there were instant lights that did not require a flame, music played from machines, and the entire ship was propelled by some enormous engine, humming continuously, day and night.

Winnie could peek over the gated barriers on deck and observe the first class passengers sipping hot broth in fine china cups. Lounging upon wooden deck chairs, the ladies wore clothing she'd seen modeled in *The Ladies Home Journal*. Each lady carried a colorful parasol, her head adorned with a plumed hat. The men wore either high domed hats called "bowlers" or round brimmed straw hats that Lizzie called "Panama hats." So different from the practical tweed cap and work clothes she was used to seeing Da wear.

Da ... a tear formed in the corner of Winnie's eye. She recalled the wrenching goodbye to Da at the rail station of Fintona. She had not been able to stop her sobs. Emily had held her arm gently but firmly, calming her with the words, "'Tis all right. The family will come join us in America, by and by."

"Take good care of Winifred, my dear Emily," Da had said.

"Of course I will," Emily had said. She had led Winnie inside the train, taking seats beside the window.

Through the open train window, the two girls had watched Da reach into the inside pocket of his old overcoat. He'd pulled out a pressed yellow rose. On one stem there was an open blossom, and below it, a new bud. Handing it to them, he had said, "'Tis from your mother, she loves you so. Be brave, my darlings. Won't be long before we come join you." At that, the train had lumbered out of the station, its cargo heavy with two young girls grieving their separation from the only world they had ever known.

Winnie reached into the pocket of her pinafore, feeling the smooth edge of Ma's letter and the prickly stem of the rose.

A motherly voice broke Winnie's reverie. "Winnie, would you like to come with us to the other side of the deck? The staff has got some games planned for the children. Sack races, and such." Winnie looked up to see Mrs. Thompson and her twelve-year-old daughter, Maggie. With curly black hair piled on the top of her head in a loose bun, Mrs. Thompson was a contrast in color to her fair haired daughter. However, they shared the same sparkling brown eyes that frequently slipped into smiling crescents. Winnie had met them at dinner several days ago. Originally from County Leitrim, they were now traveling to Newport, Rhode Island, where they'd join Mr. Thompson. A job as a nurse awaited Mrs. Thompson.

"Oh, hello, Mrs. Thompson and Maggie. Yes, I'd like to play, but I need to go down below to tell Emily and Lizzie." Winnie's face brightened at the prospect of some physical activity.

"We'll meet you at the game area. We're going to try and round up a few other children first." Mrs. Thompson and Maggie smiled, and walked along the deck to find some more playmates.

Winnie took a deep breath of ocean air, filling her lungs with fresh air before facing the rank air below. She stepped down the narrow gray metal staircase to the unmarried women's dormitory. She walked through a tight aisle, passing row after row of cold metal bunk beds. Between each stack of beds was a gray tin basin with an electric light bulb overhead illuminating a mirror. Each bed was covered by a gray wool blanket. So much gray! Finally she arrived at a set of bunk beds occupied by her sister, and above, Lizzie. Winnie saw that they were resting, looking pale and nauseous.

"Emily, Mrs. Thompson has asked if I would like to join in some games with the children up on deck. Would you like to go, too?" Winnie angled her head, waiting for Emily's reply.

"My body says 'no', but my mind tells me I've got to do something besides lie here. What do you think, Lizzie?" Emily stretched her neck to see Lizzie above her.

"Oh, you girls go without me. I've signed all of us on the registry for evening tea at seven o'clock. I'll meet you there." Lizzie smiled weakly and pulled a blanket to her chin.

"All right, Lizzie, have a rest, and we'll save you a seat at tea," Emily said. She lowered her feet onto the gray floor, slowly shifting her toes into her shoes. Smoothing the blanket and sheets of her bed, she asked Winnie, "So, you've seen your friend, Maggie, today?"

"Yes, Maggie and her mother will be at the games. Come on, Emily, they've probably started." Winnie was desperate to get out of the stench of the dormitory.

Emily pulled herself to her feet, steadying herself by hanging onto the metal bars of the bunk bed. Winnie started down the passageway at an anxious pace, Emily shuffling behind.

When they got above deck, a cold ocean breeze washed over Winnie's face, clearing away the stale air. "Over there, Emily. Let's go find the Thompsons." Winnie pointed to a crowd of passengers. There was a hum of voices and laughter as children climbed into burlap sacks and began to hop around.

"Winnie, why don't you go ahead. It's enough that I've walked up the stairs. Hopping around in a sack is more than I can manage. I'll be content to sit here and watch the fun." Emily took a seat on a bench to watch the races, pulling a shawl tightly across her shoulders.

Suddenly feeling a little bashful, Winnie edged up to greet Mrs. Thompson.

"So glad you joined the fun, Winnie! Come on over here." Mrs. Thompson pointed to a place in line behind Maggie. "This is called a relay race. When it's your turn, you'll be handed a sack, you hop along, tag the pole, and turn around to the finish line. Looks like you'll be the anchor for your team. That means you'll be finishing the race!" Mrs. Thompson stepped aside as Winnie stood in line, trying to figure out the best technique in sack racing.

There were screams of excitement as the opposing team hopped ahead of Winnie's team. The current sack hopper on Winnie's team was a small boy, about seven years old, and he had a difficult time keeping upright. He nearly rolled his way down the deck to the pole and back. He handed off the sack to an identical looking boy, with the same near transparent complexion and fair hair, presumably his twin. The twin fared slightly better, toppling over only one time. Next, it was Maggie's turn, and she had a length of deck to make up before catching the other team. Maggie took off, hopping in a confident rhythm. Winnie shouted, "Good hopping, Maggie. Keep it up!"

As Maggie turned, her blonde braids whipping wildly at the sides of her red face, she yelled, "Come on, Winnie, it's up to you: catch them!" She let the sack drop off her and without wasting a single motion, Winnie pulled the sack to her waist and took off like a jack rabbit. She used a series of lightning fast leaps to catch the opposing team. The sound of cheering teammates' voices was a blurry background to the pounding of her heart. Why did it matter so much to win? A feeling came over her, much like the time she was determined to tag Connor Quinn. Only one thought existed in her mind: win the race! Winnie pushed herself across the finish line to the boisterous cheers of her team.

"You did it! Winnie, you caught up with the other team, and you won!" Maggie pulled Winnie into the crowd of teammates. They gathered around and patted her, sweaty and laughing. For one glorious moment, Winnie let herself soak in the glow of victory.

"Where did you learn to hop like that? Is it the custom in County Tyrone to hop around in a sack all day? Or are you part rabbit?" Mrs. Thompson asked, laughing.

There were several more races, including a three legged race, and an obstacle course. Winnie forgot her homesickness for a couple of hours of running and laughing.

A tinny sounding bell rang, signaling tea time. "Is it seven o'clock already, Mrs. Thompson?" Winnie asked.

"Yes, that it is! Time for tea, thank heavens." Mrs. Thompson looked around for her belongings, a book and a shawl, and directed Maggie to go down below for tea.

"Thank you so much for telling me about the games. I had a lot of fun!" Winnie flashed a big smile. It actually felt peculiar to feel her face open up. Today was the first day during her trip that she had a genuine smile and hearty laughter.

"Winnie!" Emily called. "'Tis time for tea. Are you ready?"

"Coming, Em." Winnie picked up a sweater from a bench, no longer needing it after working up a sweat from the games. She joined Emily, and the two headed downstairs for the dining hall.

Chapter 14
Tea on the High Seas

The girls entered the long dining hall, aiming for a familiar spot. It was a small comfort to sit at the same wooden chairs for every meal. The table was covered with a bold geometric patterned cloth, and each place was set with sturdy dishes.

Lizzie had not yet arrived, and as the girls sat down, an older man greeted them. "Good evening to you, lasses," said the man, his eyes peering out of a weathered face. A vision of Da skid across Winnie's mind.

"Good evening to you," replied the girls in unison.

"Name's Mr. McDevitt. When I saw you lasses, I couldn't help but think of my own girls back in Aranmore. And what would your names be?" Again, Winnie felt an ache for Da.

"This is my sister, Winifred Weir, and I am Emily Weir." Emily reached out to shake his hand.

"Sisters! I might have guessed. And where is your destination?"

"We are heading to Stamford, Connecticut, to live with our aunt," Emily said, pouring herself some tea.

"Oh, 'tis a bright future you'll have in America. I'm off to Freeland, Pennsylvania, myself, to do a bit of farm work. My Uncle Gordy, he's got a farm there, you know, and there's lots of land. Not like Donegal. Can't squeeze a life's earnings from that land. Besides, my oldest brother, he will inherit the farm from Da. Not enough land for the rest of us, so it's off to America for me. Uncle Gordy says a man can make a decent wage, working the land. And some money to spare so my girls and their Mam can come and join me." Mr. McDevitt tipped the teapot to pour himself some lukewarm tea.

Winnie looked up, noticing Lizzie feebly making her way towards them.

As she neared them, Lizzie said, "Hello, girls! I've finally managed to get myself out of bed." She sank into the chair beside Emily.

"Lizzie, it's so good to see you here," Emily said and then remembered Mr. McDevitt. "I'd like to introduce you to Mr. McDevitt. He's traveling to Pennsylvania to work on a farm."

"Pleased to meet you, Mr. McDevitt. I'm Lizzie Askin, and I'm going to Brooklyn, New York." Lizzie half stood to shake hands with him.

"Then the three of you are not traveling together?" he asked.

"Well, you could say we're together for the ship ride. The girls' father has asked that I look after them on the ship, as we were acquaintances back at home." Lizzie smiled fondly at Emily and Winnie. "'Tis an easy job, I might add. Sometimes, I wonder who is looking after whom. I've been so put out by stomach ailments, I really am not much of a help."

"Well, now, what you really need are some of these biscuits. Tea, biscuits, and a lot of fresh air, I say. That's the remedy for the sickness." Mr. McDevitt, placed two biscuits upon his plate and passed the basket along to Lizzie.

"Ah, yes, well I suppose I must try to eat. 'Tis a good thing this is not a long trip. What have we got . . . just three more days?" Lizzie asked as she counted the days on her fingers.

"Well, the stewards have been saying that we've taken a bit longer this journey, thanks to the rough seas, you may have noticed. 'Twill be four more days, give or take a day." Mr. McDevitt bit down upon the hard biscuit and began to chew laboriously. "Need to wash this down with a spot of tea!" He emptied his teacup in one gulp and wiped his mouth with the napkin with a less than satisfied look. "I do miss my wife's cooking."

"I suppose we all miss something. But the important thing is look ahead to the future. Isn't that right, girls?" Lizzie tilted her strong chin towards Emily and Winnie, and they nodded, wide-eyed, but not convinced.

Emily glanced towards an approaching family. "Look, Winnie. Aren't those boys coming this way the twins who were on your sack race team?" She tried to politely indicate two tow-headed boys, following their mother and a younger brother.

"Yes, they are. Their names are Gerald and Terry McKay, and the wee lad behind them is Adrian. Of course, that's their ma, Mrs. McKay." Winnie caught Mrs. McKay's eyes, and waving, she motioned to the unoccupied seats next to her.

Everyone at the table stood up and introduced themselves to the McKays.

"Hello, yes, Winnie, isn't it? You certainly make a fine sack racer!" Mrs. McKay had the same translucent skin and white-blonde hair as her three children, and she beamed a wide smile as she spoke.

"Well, come now, have a seat and join us," Mr. McDevitt said, pulling out a chair for Mrs. McKay.

"Thank you so much, Mr. McDevitt. Children, have a seat." Mrs. McKay settled in Adrian and motioned the boys to bow their heads to pray with her. Winnie felt another pang of homesickness, thinking of her family table and the blessings Da had prayed. She closed her eyes with the McKays and silently made her own prayer for a speedy reunion with her family.

Gerald and Terry drank cream from their teacups, and showed no interest in eating. Little Adrian kept lunging towards the salt shaker, with Mrs. McKay interrupting him.

She blocked Adrian's hand just as he was within an inch of the shaker. "No, Adrian. I've told you before, it is not good for you to eat so much salt!" She looked up at the amused faces of her table companions and explained, "Some have a sweet tooth, but my Adrian, he must have been born with a salt tooth! You should see how he favors the bacon at breakfast."

The twins were getting restless and began to entertain themselves by poking each other. Gerald pulled Terry's hair, and Terry squealed in exaggerated agony.

"He hurt me, Ma!" Terry shouted, and then twirled around and swatted Gerald's arm.

"Ma, Terry's hitting me!" Gerald had a look of total innocence upon his face.

"Now, boys," Mrs. McKay said, looking around, blushing in embarrassment, "Try to behave. This is no place for a fight."

Both boys folded their arms angrily and pouted, furrowing their identical brows accusingly at each other.

Lizzie, sensing an imminent storm, said, "Boys, I don't suppose you can read?"

"Of course, we can. Finished the first class in Dalry. That's in Scotland. And we even got started in second class," Terry said proudly.

"Well, in that case, I wonder if you'd like to read some comic strips from an American newspaper?" Lizzie slowly opened her handbag, purposely building suspense, then drew out a folded newspaper with a flourish of her long arms. Terry and Gerald watched in utter amazement.

Lizzie unfolded the paper, shook out the folds, and cleared her throat. She held it up for everyone to see and read the title with a voice of authority; "The Captain and the Kids."

"Well, now boys, what do you say to Miss Askin?" Mrs. McKay looked at her boys, prompting them with her elbow.

"Ah . . . thank you!" Gerald barked, grabbing at the paper.

Terry lunged for the paper at the same moment, but Mrs. McKay intercepted the paper comics. She swept the paper above her head, out of their reach. Her face went from pearl white to crimson. She said, "That's enough, boys!" Turning to Lizzie, her face pinched in exhaustion, she added, "Thank you so much for the diversion. Heaven knows we need one! 'Twill make for some interesting bedtime reading."

Winnie watched as Mrs. McKay gathered up a sleepy Adrian. She fit his droopy head into the crook of her neck, her forearm supporting his bottom. Winnie thought how the mother and child fit together like the pieces of cut fabric Ma would stitch together to sew a pinafore. Winnie swallowed hard as she realized she could not conjure an image of Ma's frail arms holding wee Tommy. Next came an image of Da cradling five-year-old William's lifeless body.

"Let me help you with your things," Lizzie said, standing to help. She stacked a few biscuits on a cloth napkin, tying up the ends, and handed it to Gerald. "There you go. A bedtime snack, just in case." Gerald took the bundle from Lizzie and reached for his mother's free hand.

"That's lovely, thank you." Mrs. McKay pulled Gerald along and nodded for Terry to follow. As they walked down the dining hall aisle, Terry and Gerald resumed their fussing about who would get to read the comics first.

Mr. McDevitt chortled, shaking his head. "She's got her hands full! 'Tis a difficult thing to journey with three young ones."

"That it is." Lizzie took a last sip of tea, and turned to Emily and Winnie. "Well, I suppose a stroll on deck would be in order now. I feel a little strength returning to my aching limbs."

Winnie and Emily nodded and stood, bidding Mr. McDevitt goodnight.

Lizzie, Emily, and Winnie maneuvered through the dining hall and up the steps to a view of the North Atlantic night sky. The crisp air smelled of the sea.

"Do you think it's true that your wish will come true if you wish upon the first star you see at night?" Winnie asked Emily.

"It couldn't hurt to try," Emily said. Winnie shut her eyes and wished so hard she thought her head would burst.

"You know girls, I'd like to tell you a little about what lies ahead for you. If Mr. McDevitt is correct, in four days we shall arrive in New York Harbor. 'Twill be a glorious sight. The Statue of Liberty. The skyscrapers. The motor cars, the electric trolleys. People from all over the earth living together." Lizzie had a dreamy look.

Wrapped in the inky blackness of the night, with the sound of the waves splashing up against the side of the California, Winnie was hypnotized.

"You will need to go through inspection at Ellis Island. Don't let that worry you. You'll pass without problems. It's people like that poor Ellen McGhee who should be worried. Poor thing, she's been coughing up a storm since the day she set foot on this ship. Looks like a ghost. Your friend's mother, Mrs. Thompson, she's a nurse, and she says Ellen's got the cough of that awful tuberculosis. As sorry as it is, you must keep your distance. Don't want to get infected yourself, girls."

"What will happen to Ellen if she is ill when we arrive in America?" Emily asked.

"She'll probably be hospitalized. Either that, or deported. Sent back from where she came. 'Tis a sad thing to think on." Lizzie pulled her hair away from her face wistfully.

Winnie peered between the hanging lifeboats that lined the rail and over the edge, down to the black ocean below. A view of the sheer drop down the side of the ship to the icy water, sent a chill up her spine. "Emily, let's go inside. I'm cold and tired."

"Of course, Winnie. You've had a long day, what with the sack races and all." Emily tightened her grip on her shawl. "Lizzie, are you coming?"

"In a moment, girls. I'll see you downstairs after I've had a few more moments to ponder the future." Lizzie stood tall, taking in a deep breath.

Preparations for bed were difficult for Winnie. There was so little privacy, and always a long line of passengers waiting to use the tiny water closet that reeked of unmentionable odors. Winnie would pass the time waiting in line imagining herself hovering above the crowd, a winged fairy with magical powers. She'd be able to fly back to Corbally and watch her family going about their daily business. Then she realized that she'd miss Emily, and was more than a little curious about America. Winifred the fairy would glide back to check on Emily's progress on the California. That would suit her just fine. A little of both worlds.

With a hasty visit to the water closet completed, Winnie hurried down the aisle to her bunk. She had a special way of slipping out of her clothes and into her night gown without ever exposing bare skin. Emily stood before the mirror, brushing out her hair. Winnie couldn't be bothered; she'd take care of her hair in the morning. For now, she'd curl up with a copy of "Buster Brown" comics that

Lizzie had left on her bed. Tomorrow she'd share the comics with Maggie.

Emily finished her hair brushing and pulled out a paper and pen. She was writing a letter to Ma, adding to it each night. Winnie noticed a single tear track down Emily's cheek.

A thought occurred to Winnie and she leaned out of her bed, groping for her luggage beneath. She'd carelessly stuffed her pinafore into the luggage, but had forgotten something in the pocket. With relief, Winnie pulled out Ma's letter and read it for the hundredth time:

My Dearest Winifred,

You are now embarking upon the journey of a lifetime. May God bless you and guide you.

Long ago when I was a young girl, my mother forbid me from eating the lovely pastries the servants had set out on the dining room table. They were to be served to my Da's very important visitors. I pouted and stomped my feet. When no one was looking I broke off a corner of a pastry and ran out the back door. Stuffing the pastry into my mouth, I was disappointed at how dry and tasteless it was. I threw the rest of the crust to the swans and sat down in the pasture. To my surprise, the grass was littered with wild strawberries. To this day, I will never forget how sweet those sun-warmed berries tasted, far better than any pastry.

Be brave, make your family proud, and know that we pray for you daily.

Love,
Ma and Da

Chapter 15
Three Boys, One Dog, a Storm, and a Brave Girl

The next morning, breakfast followed the same routine Winnie had come to expect. Tea that was neither hot nor strong enough, toast with marmalade (how she missed strawberry jam!), and hard boiled eggs that were so overcooked the yolks were green. There was bacon as well, but the white gristle made Winnie's stomach turn.

Seated at her table this morning were some young ladies Lizzie had befriended in their dormitory. Winnie had hoped to see Maggie this morning, but she must have eaten breakfast at the earlier seating. The conversations around her were full of optimistic plans for future life in America. While most of the travelers were coming as domestic servants, some would be seamstresses, cooks, and nurses. And the places they were traveling to! America had such strange names for places, thought Winnie. Philadelphia, Schenectady, San Francisco. Voices bounced back and forth across the table. Suddenly, Winnie realized that someone was addressing her.

"Are you traveling to America to be a Bridget?" Winnie looked up to see a young lady with auburn hair and a face sprinkled with freckles.

Winnie did not know what to say. What was a Bridget? She shook her head and said, "Oh no, I am going to live my aunt until my ma and da come with the rest of the family soon enough."

She replied, "Isn't that lovely! Well, I am going to Philadelphia to be a Bridget myself. 'Tis an opportunity to make something of myself." Several tables away, a handsome young man waved at the young lady. Her face brightened in recognition and she stood to leave. "Well, I wish you well in America," she said, leaving to join her male acquaintance at his table.

Emily was just finishing one last bite of a rubbery egg, when Winnie caught her attention. "Em, what did that lady mean when she asked if I was a Bridget?"

Emily smiled, and explained, "Oh, that is just a way some people describe an Irish servant girl. But of course, Aunt Mabel is family, and she is going to treat us like her own. We will have chores, just like we had at home, but we'll be American ladies. Don't worry, Winnie."

But Winnie could not let go of the idea. "Why did the shipmaster write 'Servant' as your occupation?"

"Oh, Winnie, he had to write something in the empty space, didn't he? Besides, we owe Aunt Mabel something since she did pay for our passage. Never you mind, the shipmaster did not write 'servant' in your space. In America, children your age are not allowed to be employed in that way. See how lucky you are to be going to America?"

Winnie was not convinced of her good fortune.

The ship lurched and the breakfast dishes rattled and slipped a few inches on the tables.

"'Tis a rough sea today, girls," Lizzie said. "I was out this morning and the sky is working itself up to a bit of a storm. We'll have to pass the time down below." Lizzie sighed and took the napkin off her lap, placing it upon the table. "Are you ready to back to the dormitory, girls?"

"Yes, I suppose there's nothing else to do." Disappointment washed across Winnie's face. There would be no chance to get fresh air today.

As the three made their way down the narrow hallway, a very distraught Mrs. McKay rushed towards them from the opposite direction. "Oh, dear! It's Adrian! I've lost Adrian!" Mrs. McKay looked at them helplessly. "And once I realized Adrian had disappeared, the twins took off in search, and I've lost them as well!"

"Don't worry, we'll all help, Mrs. McKay." Lizzie put her hand across Mrs. McKay's shoulders. "Tell us where you were when you last saw everyone."

"Well, we had finished breakfast and had just gone to the family dormitory. I was having a dizzy spell, so I stepped into the water closet. As soon as I came out, I noticed that Adrian was not on the bed where I had told him to stay. Gerald and Terry were at it again, fighting in their usual manner. When I asked them where Adrian was, they had no idea. Hadn't even noticed he'd gone. And before I could stop them, they took off saying, 'We'll find him!' I tried to yell 'stop', but they just kept running. They went this way." Mrs. McKay indicated the direction towards the dining hall. She was near tears, and Lizzie steadied her with a firm hand.

"You don't have the strength to stand, poor thing. Emily, why don't you take Mrs. McKay back to her bed, while Winnie and I start searching. We'll tell the stewards and everyone we see on the way. We'll find them." Lizzie looked strong and confident. "And don't forget, I've got the fastest girl on the ship here as my helper." Lizzie patted Winnie's back, and Winnie blushed. "Let's get going, Winnie."

Lizzie seemed to feel much better today. Maybe Mr. McDevitt had been right: tea, biscuits, and fresh air. Anyway, Lizzie and Winnie had a mission to complete. They marched with purpose back to the dining hall and pulled aside the nearest steward.

"Have you seen some small blonde boys? Twins, about seven years old, and maybe a younger one, about four or five?" Lizzie asked.

The steward shook his head no and said, "Haven't seen them, but I'll keep an eye out. I'll tell the rest of the staff to look out as well."

"Thank you," Lizzie said, steering Winnie through the doorway down a hallway she'd never seen before.

"What's down here?" Winnie asked.

"I think it's storage. Listen, do you hear something?" Lizzie cocked her head and concentrated on a faint sound.

"Yes . . . could it be the sound of barking dogs?" Winnie asked.

"It very well could be. The first class passengers often travel with their dear pets." Lizzie spoke with an exaggerated English accent, her nose high in the air.

"Wait, Lizzie, don't you hear another sound as well?" Winnie scooted closer to the source. "Yes, that sounds like Gerald and Terry bickering!" Winnie turned toward to a door. "Sounds like the noise is coming from this room." She pointed at the doorknob, afraid to open it herself.

"No sense in being shy about it, we'll just go in. Let's not waste time getting permission from stewards!" Lizzie plowed forward, opening the door.

As she turned the knob, the boys' voices were joined by a high pitched yelp. Winnie and Lizzie entered the room, baffled, and were immediately faced with a leaping black Scottish terrier, determined to get past them.

"A dog!" exclaimed Winnie.

Gerald and Terry squatted before an open cage, looking extremely guilty.

"We didn't mean to let it out!" In an instant the terrier darted past Lizzie and Winnie, through the open door and down the hall.

"Chase it, Winnie!" Lizzie yelled, amidst a racket of barking.

Winnie reacted without thinking. It was just like the sack races, just like tag. She had to get that dog!

Running down the hall, she could hear the rapid beat of clicking paws upon the planks of the ship. Spying a flash of short furry legs bounding up some steps, Winnie followed, and found herself in a strange room full of peculiar machines. A lady sat upon something that resembled a bike that did not move forward, its wheels revolving endlessly. She pumped with such determination. Why would anyone waste their time on such a machine? When the lady saw Winnie, she stopped and gasped. "My goodness! You've given me a fright! First it's a dog, next a girl! Is that your dog, little girl? You'd better get it. It's against the rules to let it run free like that." The lady shook her head and resumed her endless bike journey to nowhere.

Winnie ran through the room, deciding that this might be the exercise room Lizzie had once described. Hearing a shrill yelp, she followed the sound to another strange room. There was quiet music playing, and lush carpets on the floor. All around her were velvet sofas and tall plants in ceramic pots. First class passengers stood around, smoke ringing their heads as they chatted and sipped drinks from crystal glasses. Noting a disturbance in the far corner of the room, Winnie scooted across the carpet to find the dog cornered by some angry faced men.

"Is this your dog, young lady?" A scowling older man wearing spectacles beckoned a steward. "Take this dog out of here!"

Suddenly a lady's voice shot out, "Wait! That's my Linwood! Oh, Linwood, how on earth did you get in here?" The lady looked accusingly at Winnie.

"Steward, please assist Mrs. Prescott and her dog." The scowling man turned to face Winnie. "Now, young lady, would you please explain yourself?"

"I'm very sorry, sir. I was just, you see . . . there's a lost boy, and then his brothers let out the dog."

"I suggest you run along to your people, young lady. This room is for first class passengers only." With that, the man swiveled, resuming a position among his other smoke-ringed companions.

Winnie was more than happy to leave, and as she made her way across the room she heard Mrs. Prescott fussing over Linwood. "You poor doggie. What on earth happened to you?" She examined Linwood from top to bottom, probing every inch of his furry body, much to Linwood's displeasure. Finally, she handed a squirming Linwood back to the steward. "See that there is a proper lock on his cage. And make sure Linwood gets a fresh bone from the first class kitchen." She flashed one last look of disapproval at Winnie.

The harried steward caught up with Winnie, Linwood struggling against him in his arms. "You know you are not supposed to be in here."

"Of course not, sir. I was trying to catch the dog. I am very sorry." Winnie was overwhelmed with shame for having broken a rule. She wished she could disappear, shrink into a fairy and fly home to Da.

The steward led her to the steerage deck area, and his expression changed. He looked at her kindly and said, "Don't be worrying about all that. I have to enforce the rules, or I'll lose my job. First class passengers treat me with airs all the time. You'll understand when you are a little older. Anyway, Mrs. Prescott ought to be thanking you for finding her dear doggie." Winnie looked at Linwood who stared back with dark wide eyes. She decided that she liked this dog, even if he had caused her so much trouble.

The steward grinned at Linwood, and then at Winnie. "I think you've made a friend." Thunder rumbled and he looked up at the heavy clouds overhead. "You need to take cover. Do you know where your Ma is?" Winnie winced at the mention of Ma, but did not take the time to explain.

"Yes, sir." She bent her head as prickling rain began to fall.

Winnie chose the closest door, although she really wasn't exactly sure where she was on the ship. There was yet another long corridor lined with closed doors. Sooner or later, she'd recognize something. She felt utterly defeated, not having found Adrian and having broken so many rules. She'd just have to go back and tell Mrs. McKay the bad news and hope that someone else had found Adrian. Just as she rounded a bend in the hall, she thought she heard a man's voice in distress. Stopping to listen, she recognized the steward's voice, although the words he was yelling could not be repeated. Why was he so agitated? Winnie got her answer in the form of the clickety-clack of Linwood's claws upon the floor. Linwood had made another get away, and he was headed straight for her.

Winnie squatted down with open arms and called, "Here, Linwood, here you go, old boy." Linwood had other ideas. Streaking past her, he used his stout snout to push open one of the doors. He seemed to know exactly where he was going.

Winnie peered inside, afraid to enter a forbidden room again. This was another storage room, and Linwood was nosing around a crate that appeared to have toppled over. Dancing in circles around the crate, he alternated barks with excited sniffs of something scattered about the floor.

"Linwood, what is it?" Winnie rushed towards Linwood, who looked up at her almost as if he were trying to tell her something. Joining in his loud noise was a high pitched screech. Was that a young child crying?

She peered sideways into the dark crate, and low and behold, there was the very blonde top of Adrian's head. And he was wedged inside, waist high in bacon!

"Adrian, you poor thing! Let me get you out of this awful

place!" Winnie reached deep inside and used all her strength to pull him by his armpits. The rocking motion of the ship made it even more difficult to keep her balance, but she managed to dig him out. Adrian was absolutely bawling by now, frightened of Linwood, and not quite sure of Winnie.

A moment later, the steward entered the room and called, "Halloo! Anyone in here? Is that you, Linwood, you naughty dog?"

"Yes, sir, 'tis Linwood and I," Winnie said hesitantly. Kneeling with a greasy, red-faced Adrian and a yelping Linwood, she braced herself for his wrath.

"Well, as I live and breathe, I have never seen such a sight!" The steward broke into uproarious laughter and Winnie had no choice but to join him, out of relief. Adrian just bawled even louder.

"You three sure make a sight! If only Mrs. Prescott could see her dear doggie now. Up to his tail in bacon!" The steward bent down to grab Linwood, but the dog snarled at him, baring his fangs. "Steady, boy, we'll have none of that!" The dog would not let the steward close.

"Let me try," Winnie said as she sat down. In a very quiet voice she cooed, "Here boy, come here." She patted her lap, and sure enough Linwood leapt into her lap, as if he'd been doing this every day of his life. Winnie gently stroked his wavy black fur, and speaking softly to him, she slowly stood up, balancing him in her arms. Linwood nuzzled his snout against Winnie's neck.

"I suppose it takes a feminine touch," said the steward, shaking his head and taking off his cap to wipe the sweat from his brow. "I think I'll have you escort our furry friend back to his cage. But what shall we do about the young fellow?"

Adrian's screams had faded into the background, and Winnie had nearly forgotten him as he sat, crimson shiny-faced beside the crate. Winnie said, "Let me see what I can do."

Winnie knelt before the wailing child and quietly said, "Adrian, look at the dog. He's asking you to stop crying." Adrian paused to check if Linwood was actually speaking words. When he realized the dog could not truly talk, he began to cry again, but not with the same fervor.

"If you come with me, I'll take you back to your Ma. She's awfully worried about you." Winnie reached out with a free hand and raised Adrian to his feet.

Adrian mumbled, "My tummy hurts." And, much to his and Winnie's dismay, he vomited all over the floor.

Winnie certainly had seen her share of sickness during the trip.

The steward said, "You take care of the dog and the boy. I have more than a little experience with cleaning up this kind of mess." He steward pulled a cloth from his back pocket and dabbed at Adrian's face. "There you go, off to your Ma." Looking up at Winnie, he added, "The dog crates are kept two doors down on the right. I'll follow to check on the lock, but you'd best be off right now." Pulling a mop and bucket from a closet, the steward smiled. "You've done well for yourself today, young lady."

Winnie flushed in pride and guided Adrian down the hall. Linwood had practically melted into her arms, and she was reluctant to tuck him away in his cage.

Adrian had quieted down, now that he was rid of the bacon in his stomach, and he walked beside Winnie all the way back to the family dormitory. The storm had subsided and the ship felt more stable.

"You've found him!" Mrs. McKay rushed over to Adrian from the narrow space between bunks where she had been pacing. She lifted him to her cheek.

"Winnie, we were so worried about you, too. You've been gone for over an hour!" Emily said, looking very relieved and slightly curious. "Where did you find Adrian?"

Winnie told the story as everyone nearby gathered around. She tried to tell the story as Da would have: embellishing details, exaggerating Linwood's narrow escapes, choosing just the right words. It was a good tale.

"Didn't I tell you Winnie would save the day?" Lizzie said, patting Winnie on the back.

"'Tis no surprise to me. Winnie's a very brave girl," said Emily.

Chapter 16
A Change of Name

During the next three days, time aboard the ship dragged like a reluctant mule. The excitement of having found Linwood and returning Adrian faded into the monotonous routines of meals and passing time. Winnie wished she could have spent more time with Maggie, but as Mrs. Thompson was a nurse, the two volunteered their help among steerage passengers with minor ailments. Mrs. Thompson said that Maggie was her best assistant. Many of the passengers in the family dormitory were plagued with head lice, and Mrs. Thompson taught mothers how to nit-pick children's hair with a fine tooth comb. The McKay twins were forever scratching their heads, their white blonde hair sticking out wildly in all directions. And there were lots of whispers about one young Swedish passenger in the dormitory for unmarried women. One night, Lizzie and Mrs. Thompson were speaking in hushed voices, but stopped when Winnie had come down the aisle. When Winnie begged Emily to tell, she shrugged and said, "There are just some things better left to the grownups." Winnie had peeked at the Swedish woman frequently, but she seemed only to be suffering from the same nausea as the rest of them. Yet there was a sunken look to her eyes that reminded Winnie of Ma and her weariness.

Winnie herself began to struggle with worse seasickness, as sanitary conditions in steerage deteriorated. The odor alone made her throat tighten in dry spasms, her stomach churning.

On the day before the scheduled arrival in New York, Winnie had spent the morning resting upon her bed, unable to gather the strength to go to the dining hall for dinner at one o'clock.

At her bunk, Emily set down her crocheting and said, "Come along, Winnie, 'tis dinnertime. Lizzie has already gone ahead." She held out a hand and pulled Winnie to her feet.

Winnie sniffed as Emily led her down the passageway. "Smells like fish today, or is that someone's breakfast second time 'round?"

"Don't be so awful, Winnie. At least we can have some bread and sip tea."

"Well, I miss our tea, I miss our toast, our table, our chairs, our Ma, our Da . . ." The words flooded from Winnie's tense mouth and she broke into tears.

Emily brushed Winnie's chestnut hair from her face. "There, there, I know 'tis hard." The girls stood before the narrow stairs, holding onto the rail, steadying themselves as the ship lurched.

"Winnie, my heart is as heavy as yours. But we must carry on. As Da said, you have to be a grown lady now. Aunt Mabel is expecting a fourteen year old, and you must do everything you can to act older than you are. I just know you can, Winnie. Do it for Da."

Winnie collected herself with a deep breath and proceeded up the stairs, still hanging onto Emily's warm fingers.

They sat down in their usual spots. Winnie felt a little self-conscious about her swollen red eyes. Maggie and Mrs. Thompson were already seated at the table, and there was a buzz in the air. Excited voices talked about arriving in New York.

Maggie turned towards Winnie and held her forearm. "Winnie, isn't it so exciting that tomorrow we will arrive in New York?!" Her crescent eyes crinkled as she smiled.

Winnie wished she could share Maggie's excitement, but all she felt was envy. Maggie already had her ma and was about to be reunited with her da.

"Winnie," Maggie continued, "you haven't said much about your plans. Now who was it you said would be meeting you in New York?"

Winnie explained about Aunt Mabel, her boarding house, and the markets. She had to admit to herself that it all sounded rather sophisticated. Maggie appeared impressed.

Platters filled with pale fish stew were passed from one person to the next. The lack of fresh air and exercise combined with the dizzying rhythmic motion of the ship did little to build an appetite. Winnie sipped her tea and nibbled some dry white bread.

Emily nodded to Winnie, and they rose to leave.

"Girls, before you leave, let me tell you something. There is talk of a 'crossroads' dance tonight. Please join us on deck at sundown!" Mrs. Thompson said.

"Sounds like fun, doesn't it, Winnie?" Emily nudged Winnie.

"Oh . . . ah, yes!" Winnie said, shaking her head a little too rigorously to make up for her lack of enthusiasm.

"Let's go down below and make sure our bags are packed properly. Then we can get ready for the dance." Emily seemed excited about the plan and Winnie shuffled behind her.

When they arrived at their bunks, Winnie's legs buckled in weariness. "I just need to lie down, Em. I might feel better if I have a nap." No one was sleeping well at night in the dormitories. There was always the noise of someone moving about to use the water closet, and the electric lights were never fully turned off.

"Very well," Emily nodded. "Take a little nap, and I will wake you in about an hour." She looked deep into Winnie's eyes, with such affection and concern, that for one fleeting moment Winnie thought she was looking into Da's blue eyes.

"Thanks, Em." She flipped onto her side and pulled up the gray blanket.

Deep sleep inhabited by dreams of green pastures swept Winnie away. But in no time at all, Emily was tapping her shoulder.

"Winnie, are you awake?" Emily set aside the letter she was writing and watched Winnie stir.

"Yes, I was just dreaming of collecting eggs from Clucky. Do you think Annie has taken over my chore?"

"I doubt that she can collect eggs with a broken leg, but I am sure Ma and Da are managing just fine. Clucky, on the other hand, must miss being chased by you."

"I wish I was Annie," Winnie said frowning, propping herself up in her bed.

"Now why would a pretty girl like Winnie want to be anybody else but herself?" Emily asked.

"Well, first off . . . Annie is at home with Ma and Da, and next, I hate the name Winnie!"

"I don't think there is anything we can do about your first complaint, but surely we can do something about the latter," Emily said.

"What do you mean?" Winnie blinked.

"Well, I suppose if you dislike your name, we could give you a new name, now that you will be an American."

"Do you really think I could change my name?" Winnie sat upright in the bed, narrowing her eyes in skepticism as she listened to Emily.

"Well, to be safe, you should use your given name with the authorities, but we can change your first name immediately and start using it among ourselves as you please. Now what name do you fancy?"

"Oh, Emily, could I really change my name? I have always fancied my middle name, Evelyn. 'Tis so much more grown-up and elegant. Would you call me Evelyn from now on?" Winnie shed her doubts and dropped her feet to the side of the bed.

"Absolutely! In fact, from this moment forward you shall be known as Evelyn Weir. No more little girl Winnies around here. Have you seen Winnie? Oh no, she is long gone. Last seen rolling down the grassy hills of Corbally. But may I interest you in a lovely young lady named Evelyn? She is new to these parts, but she is ever so refined."

Winnie-turned-Evelyn and Emily burst into giggles.

"I love my new name!" Evelyn's full cheeks pulled up into a wide smile.

"Evelyn, let's finish our packing, get dressed, and then go up on deck." Emily reached under her bunk and pulled out her luggage. "Let's try out your new name!"

Emily folded up her crocheting and placed her clothing inside her open bag. Evelyn did the same, although not quite as neatly. She took one extra moment to make sure the rose and Ma's letter were deep within the pocket of a folded pinafore. The nap had restored some physical strength, but her name change had given her hope.

Smoothing out the blanket, Evelyn quickly slipped her best pinafore over her head. She slithered out of her old clothes and let the pinafore drop around her. This was the dress her mother had worked on those last days in Corbally. It was also the dress she had worn as she said good bye to Da at the train station of Fintona. Evelyn would not allow herself to fall into sad thoughts, and pushed her feet into her Sunday shoes.

"Ready, Em?" Evelyn looked up at Emily who was radiant, although somewhat thinner and paler. Emily had a serene confidence that made Evelyn feel warm and protected.

The two walked past the rows of metal bunks, hand in hand, as was their habit. They emerged from the lower quarters to meet a crystal blue late afternoon sky. The breeze carried a hint of new beginnings.

Lizzie approached them with a broad smile and a sparkle in her eyes. "Can't you just smell the promise of America?"

"Lizzie, I'm so glad we found you. We've had a change of names recently, and Winnie is now to be called 'Evelyn,'" Emily said, smiling while she nudged her sister.

"Isn't that a lovely name for a lovely lass! Quite grown up and quite American, I might add," Lizzie said, standing tall above the girls. Evelyn thought how she resembled the pictures she'd seen of the Statue of Liberty. "Let me tell you what my friend Sarah was told me: tomorrow the inspectors will come on board for the first and second class passengers and of course, the rest of us will have to wait. But 'twon't be long . . . we'll be inspected at Ellis Island. 'Twill be wonderful to see New York City, don't you think?"

"Oh, yes," Emily nodded. "What shall we do to prepare?"

"Mostly, you need to be patient. These things take time. Just be ready to answer many questions and make sure you step lively. Don't want the medical examiners to think you're limp or ill. Nothing sadder than a deportation." Lizzie tucked her hair beneath her hat as a breeze brushed by.

Evelyn thought of poor Ellen McGhee, who had disappeared from the dormitory. Mrs. Thompson had assured her that Ellen was recovering in the ship's hospital room. Then there was that Swedish woman and her secret . . .

"Of course, you won't have to worry about being deported . . . it really doesn't happen much since the ship companies have done most of the inspecting at Londonderry. You see, America doesn't want anyone coming along with a dreaded disease, mental weakness, or problem that makes the immigrant a burden to the government; that or a political enemy. Don't you fret, Evelyn, you are the picture of health!" Lizzie cupped Evelyn's chin in her hand.

It suddenly occurred to Evelyn that here was her opportunity to return to Ma and Da. Could she pretend to be gravely ill or weak of mind? She was immediately ashamed for entertaining such a dishonest and cowardly thought.

The sound of an accordion interrupted Evelyn's thoughts.

"Oh, listen girls, the musicians are tuning up!" Lizzie pointed to a group of Irish steerage passengers sitting together on a bench, holding various instruments. There was a fiddler, a piper, and an accordion player.

"Let's get closer, Emily and Evelyn," Lizzie said, exaggerating the new name with drama. She pulled the girls towards a cleared area on deck. "It's just like a crossroads dance back at home! Shall we dance?"

Laughing, Lizzie began to do some Irish step dancing. Mrs. Thompson and Maggie jigged towards Lizzie, and Mrs. McKay stepped into the circle with Adrian. Mr. McDevitt pulled both Gerald and Terry into the ring, who were too stunned to continue their customary bickering. The boys' disheveled flaxen hair stood on end, having been rearranged by little scratching hands. The music was so lively, the atmosphere so gay, that Evelyn and Emily couldn't help but move their feet to the rhythm. Swept away by the laughter and hopeful faces of their fellow passengers, the girls danced long after the sun went down.

Just when Evelyn was sure she'd had enough dancing, she noticed the same steward who had shared her adventure with Linwood. He appeared to be looking for someone. Feeling emboldened by a night of dancing, not to mention her name change, she edged towards the steward, catching his eye.

"Aye! Just the young lady I was looking for." The steward waved to Evelyn, who smiled shyly.

Curious, Emily caught up to Evelyn and listened to the steward talking to her sister.

"Well, lass, seeing as how this is your last night aboard the ship, I thought you might want to bring your Ma and your friends down below to visit an old acquaintance." He grinned mischievously, waiting for Evelyn's reply.

"I . . . uh, I'm not sure who you mean," Evelyn replied, hesitating. His mistaking Lizzie for Ma sent a jolt through her body.

"Oh, come on, you've got an admirer pining away for you down below in a storage room. Howling away all night for his beloved." The steward gave a full belly laugh.

"Linwood! Oh, could we? I mean, we won't be breaking any rules, will we?" Evelyn patted down her hair as a night breeze grazed her head.

"Let's just say that it is all clear with me, and I have some influence around the storage areas."

"I'd love to invite Emily and Lizzie, if I could. Maybe Maggie and Mrs. Thompson. Too bad the McKays have gone down to the dormitory already."

"Sounds good to me. Gather everyone and I'll be waiting here." The steward turned to face the ocean, looking out at the great sea. Along the horizon, points of lights twinkled.

Evelyn coaxed Maggie, Mrs. Thompson, and Lizzie to stop dancing and join her. They followed the steward through a maze of dimly lit hallways, until they came to a door that nearly vibrated with the sound of barking dogs. Floating above the sound was an even louder, more pitiful wail.

"That particular noise, the one that sounds like weeping, why, that's your friend. Hasn't been the same since the day he met you." The steward opened the door and the group bustled in as discreetly as possible.

Evelyn bent down to the cage that produced the most melancholy lament, and beheld the black wet nose of Linwood. The steward took out a long key, unlocked the cage, and let Evelyn pull out a quivering Linwood. The dog instantaneously silenced, nuzzling her hand with his snout. Holding him in her lap, she stroked his wavy fur as everyone admired the magic she held over this dog.

"Isn't he a sweet little thing?" Lizzie asked, kneeling in closer to Linwood.

"He isn't such a sweet little thing when dealing with the likes 'o me," chortled the steward.

"Oh, he doesn't look like he could hurt a fly," Emily said, admiring his shiny black fur. Maggie and Mrs. Thompson nodded in agreement.

Beaming, Evelyn raised her index finger to her lips, indicating quiet. Linwood had nearly fallen asleep under her spell. The steward nodded that it was time to go. "Don't want you up too late on the night before your first day in America. But I know Linwood sure appreciated a 'good-bye' from you." With a sleepy Linwood tucked safely away in his crate, the steward reached to shake Evelyn's hand. He paused and said, "By the way, I don't believe I know your name, young lady."

"My name is Evelyn," she said, smiling from ear to ear.

Chapter 17
Ellis Island
October 19, 1909

Very few passengers aboard the California slept that night. Anticipation of a new life ahead had the same effect as too much strong tea. Evelyn watched as fellow passengers did their best to wash up in basins of precious little fresh water provided by the ship. Most travelers had reserved a special outfit for their day of arrival, but despite their best efforts, the ten days' worth of crowded and less than clean conditions had caused a stench that permeated everything, including the luggage.

Evelyn would have to wear the same pinafore from the night before, since it was her best, albeit wrinkled and somewhat stained. Hopefully, Aunt Mabel would understand. Closing her eyes, Evelyn could not picture Mabel's face smiling or looking remotely understanding. Shivering, she decided it best to set aside all bad thoughts and think positively, as Lizzie would say.

After a hasty breakfast, the steerage class passengers hurried to the deck area with suitcases in hand. Standing in a long line through the corridor, Evelyn could hear an audible gasp as each person emerged onto the deck. When it was her turn, she understood. Before her was a glorious sight: the skyline of New York City, with a giant verdigris lady greeting the ship's passengers.

"'Tis unbelievable!" Emily squeezed Evelyn's hand and gaped. Spying a space at the rail, the girls tucked themselves between other passengers vying for a good view.

Passengers cheered and hugged one another, their enthusiasm

warming the damp October air.

Evelyn heard someone shout, "Halloo!" and turned to see Mr. McDevitt tossing his tweed cap into the air, greeting Miss Liberty. Evelyn giggled. She couldn't help but share in the excitement.

The steam engine of the California fell silent, and in a flurry of busy movement, the ship crew prepared the ship to drop anchor in the New York Harbor. Meanwhile, a small vessel filled with inspectors approached the steamship.

Emily and Evelyn watched as the men in dark uniforms with matching flat topped hats boarded the ship. They disappeared among the first and second class passengers in a separate area hidden from view.

"What happens next?" asked Evelyn anxiously.

"We must wait our turn. I think another boat is coming for us," Emily said. Sure enough, an empty barge was making its way towards the steamship.

The ship's crew did their best to organize the steerage passengers for boarding the barge, calling out names and handing out white cards with numbers on them. There was a lot of pushing and jostling. The sisters chose to hang back and let the more aggressive passengers get ahead.

"Ouch, someone's stepped on my foot!" Evelyn could barely breathe as a tide of passengers pushed towards an opening in the railing leading to the ramp.

"Hang onto my hand. Let's stay out of the way until the crowd has gone on. No sense in trying to push ahead. Won't make any difference." For one scary moment, Emily lost hold of Evelyn's hand as the force of the crowd pushed her away. Somehow, she groped through the sea of bodies, finding the very edge of Evelyn's wool coat, drawing her in towards her like a fisherman reeling in a prized catch.

Finally, the crowd thinned to a more manageable size and the sisters stepped forward to disembark, taking a place on a crowded barge. Leaving the California, Evelyn glanced over her shoulder and thought how, despite the discomforts, she had come to regard this ship as a village populated by friends, and maybe even as a substitute home.

Aboard the barge, Evelyn again felt the unpleasant sensation of bodies surging around her, without an inch of room to spare. Because of her shorter stature, she was nearly crushed in the throng. She clung to Emily. Bodies pressed in on her from every direction; the Irish wool of her outerwear was too warm. She was drenched in anxious sweat.

"This is dreadful!" Emily said, her grip tightening on Evelyn's arm.

"Don't let me go, Em." Evelyn looped her fingers inside of Emily's grip. She grimaced and held her breath against the body odors from the swarm of unwashed bodies surrounding her. Maybe Lizzie could explain what would happen next. "Where is Lizzie?"

"I think she got on a barge ahead of this one. You know, height has its advantages." Emily forced a grin.

For what seemed an eternity, the barge chugged its way closer to a building. Evelyn found a crack between bodies through which she could see a building resembling a festive wedding cake, its striped towers festooned with green baroque turrets. But unlike a whimsical frosted cake, this building stood staunch with its serious purpose of sorting out millions of immigrants to America, not all with happy outcomes.

Unfortunately, the inspectors were overtaxed in their job of checking thousands of immigrants each day, and Evelyn and Emily once again had to wait another hour on the barge. In their cramped standing position, they held hands, quietly singing songs Ma and Da had taught them a lifetime ago.

At long last, it was the Weir sisters' turn to disembark the barge. A man on the pier shouted, "Men this way! Women and children this way!" With legs numb from standing, Evelyn and Emily were forced to hurry off to the next crowded line.

A stern eagle adornment on the facade of the building caught Evelyn's eye. She shuddered and quickly obeyed the Ellis Island employee's commands.

Heaping their suitcases in the baggage room, the girls heard a voice above the din of the crowd.

"Evelyn! Emily! Thank God you're here. Come this way!" Lizzie was waving her long arms high above.

As the girls approached, Lizzie reached out to pull them into line beside her. "I was so panicked when I couldn't find you on the barge. Now then, this is the line for women and children. Stay close to me, girls. There are lots of unsavory characters around, pickpockets and the like." Evelyn exchanged a look of alarm with

Emily, but the swarm of immigrants behind her shoved her forward.

"'Tis as if we are nothing more than a herd of cattle being led to slaughter," Evelyn whispered to Emily.

Emily's face was red, her forehead striped with worry. "Just keep moving, Evelyn. "'Twill be all right." She tightened her grip on Evelyn's sweaty hand.

Ahead in line, Mrs. McKay balanced Adrian in one arm and enclosed the twins into the folds of her bulky coat. Gerald and Terry were actually quiet, having spent their energy on relentless scratching and bickering, their slight bodies inclined against their mother.

"Girls, 'tis important to step lively and look healthy. The medical examiners are watching us, even now, as we walk up these stairs." Lizzie whispered to the girls, and Evelyn noted the bespectacled doctors discreetly watching the gait of each immigrant.

"If they see any sign of infirmity, they will pull you out for further tests. Step ahead," Lizzie said.

"Look, Emily, there is that Swedish lady. Why are the doctors pulling her aside?" Evelyn stared as a matron, the physician's helper, pulled the woman aside and marked the back of her coat in chalk with a "Pg."

Lizzie said, "Do not concern yourself. 'Tis not fit for children to meddle with others' problems."

Evelyn glanced at Emily, who shook her head. "Just move ahead and look your best, Evelyn."

When the McKays had their turn with the physician, she could hear a small commotion as the matron picked through Gerald's scalp. Both he and Terry had a chalk "Sc" on the backs of their coats. "Sc" for scalp, thought Evelyn.

"What is to become of them?" Evelyn said, her face creased in worry.

"Now, now, their problem is easy to solve. Just a bad case of head lice. They'll be taken to the medical examination room and have their little heads shaven. A douse of kerosene to their scalp, and they'll be as good as new." Lizzie let out a little snicker. "Serves them right for all the trouble they've caused their poor Ma this journey."

"But will they be separated from their Ma?" This question carried extra weight for Evelyn.

"Oh dear, no. The physicians have a heart. The family will stay together. You must understand that the physicians are here to protect America from all the problems of the old country!" Lizzie shook her head.

When it came time for Evelyn's turn to be examined, she listened carefully to the doctor's questions and answered them. She stood very still as the matron checked her heart beat. The worst part was an awful tool the doctor used to lift up her eyelids. Lizzie had warned the girls about this test. The doctors were trying to root out an incurable eye disease called "trachoma." Evelyn had watched the doctor insert a buttonhook into both Lizzie's and Emily's eyelids without causing any apparent damage, so she allowed him a look. The doctor grunted his approval, and Evelyn hurried forward to follow Lizzie and Emily.

Lizzie led them to the largest indoor space Evelyn had ever seen. Raising her voice above the din, Lizzie said, "This is the Great Hall. This is where you are registered."

What could it mean for a person to be registered to a country? Evelyn had registered for dinner on the ship, but to register for a country?

Lizzie guided the sisters to a seat on long benches, divided into sections by metal bars. Languages of every nation of the world could be heard as immigrants whispered in frightened voices to one another and translators called out each name. The faces of immigrants were shaded in tones ranging from pearl white to velvety black. For the first time in her life, Evelyn saw Africans and Asians. She had only seen pictures in books about people from the far reaches of the globe. The cacophony of echoing foreign voices made Evelyn think of a Bible story Da had told her, "The Tower of Babel."

Finding herself waiting once again, Evelyn entertained herself by surveying the ceiling. She thought of the eagle statue she'd spied earlier, but fancied herself to be more like the geese she'd seen overhead at Grandda Moffat's plantation. She imagined herself soaring, flying above the heads of everyone and perching herself on the circular chandeliers. The sunlight streaming through the clear arched windows beckoned her to the other side. With magic powers, she'd evaporate through the glass to the blue sky outside and fly across New York Harbor, all the way across the Atlantic Ocean, into the arms of Da.

"Emily and Winifred Weir," declared an authoritative American accented voice, breaking Evelyn's daydream. The sisters stood up and hesitated. Lizzie waited on the bench, urging them onward, "Go on, girls, 'tis your turn."

A dozen uniformed men were seated at long legged oak desks. Atop the slanted desktops were papers, lists of passengers. Lizzie had referred to these lists as the "ship's manifest." A bespectacled man looked up at the sisters and motioned somewhat impatiently for them to come forward. He proceeded to ask them similar questions they had been asked at Londonderry, when they first boarded the California.

"What is your name?"

Evelyn choked out her girlhood name, "Winifred Weir." Emily squeezed her hand in encouragement.

"What is your age?"

"Eleven, sir,"

"What is your nationality?"

"British Irish, sir."

He asked them about their destination and their aunt's plans for meeting them. He asked some strange questions about whether the girls were something called "anarchists," to which Emily confidently replied, "No, sir," whispering to Evelyn that she would explain later. Satisfied with the girls' answers, he handed them entry cards, and directed them down a flight of stairs to a room marked "Detained Passengers."

Evelyn did not like the sound of "detained," so similar to "deported." She narrowed her eyes and asked Emily, "Now what?" A pang of hunger cut through her stomach. Surely it was past dinner time.

"I think Lizzie told us that because we are considered 'minors.' That means children. We have to wait until we are met by Aunt Mabel in a special place. Lizzie said that she would probably be detained as well, since she is a woman traveling alone."

Before them was a broad set of stairs divided by banisters into three paths. Evelyn noticed one path, not hers, led to a white pillar. Here at the center path, travelers who had been dragging through the registry process now streamed ahead, their eyes set on the faces of loved ones. Shouts of joy bounced off the tiled walls as sisters, brothers, husbands, wives, sons, and daughters kissed and hugged. Suddenly Evelyn remembered what Lizzie had described one night on the ship: the kissing post, the place where travelers were met by loved ones.

Evelyn and Emily took the stairs that led to the detained passengers' waiting room, and sat upon yet another bench.

Several minutes later, Lizzie entered the room, her face beaming. "Girls, we've just about made it!" She dropped beside Emily and pulled out her entrance card. "Can you believe it? We're actually in America!"

"Yes, Lizzie, but why are we detained?" Evelyn's face pinched.

"Such a little worrier, you are, dear Evelyn. 'Tis just as Sarah described it. This is where we wait for our escorts. But if I am not mistaken, come dinner time, we are entitled to a meal here at Ellis Island. By the way, 'tis likely we shall see some more of our old friends from the California here."

No sooner had Lizzie uttered these words, than who should appear but Mrs. Thompson and Maggie.

"Well, well, we meet again!" Mrs. Thompson said merrily, towing her luggage, Maggie trotting behind her.

"This is where we are supposed to meet Da!" Maggie said, a grin expanding across her face.

An inspector stood before a tall desk that separated the detained passengers from a partitioned room. Lizzie pointed to room beyond him.

"You see, girls, in that room is where our long awaited friends and relatives are being interrogated. The inspectors have got to check them out as well. Make sure that their story matches ours." Lizzie straightened her hat. "Then, when the inspector deems it so, they come out, and we poor immigrants get to kiss them right over there, at our very own kissing post!" Lizzie pointed to a pillar supporting the ceiling.

"Ah, yes! A kissing post." Mrs. Thompson nodded her head thoughtfully.

The inspector raised some papers closer to his face, and announced, "Is there a Lizzie Askin here?"

Lizzie popped up and answered, "Yes!"

"Come forward, your escort has arrived." Lizzie burst forward, and, looking up, saw another woman. "Sarah!" The two friends collided into a hug, laughing.

"Oh, Sarah, you have to meet my good friends, Emily and Evelyn. It has been such a long journey, you'll never believe the stories!" Lizzie bubbled over in excitement, barely pausing to breathe. She hastily introduced Sarah to everyone, but took one last lingering look at the Weir girls.

"I'm going to miss you two. Mrs. Thompson, will you be able to stay with them until their aunt comes?" Mrs. Thompson nodded yes. A tear glistened in the corner of Lizzie's eye. "I've got your aunt's address and I'll send off a note in the post as soon as I am settled." She swiped a tear from beneath her eye. "Believe me, Emily, Evelyn, this is a good thing for you to do. Life in America is good." She said it with absolute conviction, hugged the girls and left with a spring in her step.

Feeling rather empty and most certainly hungry, Evelyn was relieved when a matron came to count the detained passengers for dinner. She ushered them to the cafeteria. Yet another massive room, with row after row of tables and benches, each place set with a battered tin plate and a fork. While the atmosphere was not exactly luxurious, the smell of steamy chicken was more than welcome.

The hungry travelers had just dug their forks into soft boiled chicken, when Emily caught a glimpse of some familiar faces entering the hall.

"Look, 'tis the McKays, and what a different look the twins have acquired!" Emily brought a napkin to her full mouth to cover the giggles she couldn't control. Evelyn looked up to see what was so humorous. Gerald and Terry's heads were whiter than before, having been shaved and cleansed, their ears sticking straight out of their bald heads, giving them an elfin appearance. Mrs. McKay had spotted the Thompsons and Weirs, and she waved as she approached.

"Well, well, so glad you could join us for dinner! Have you had a bit of a shave, young men?" Mrs. Thompson asked, laughing, as the McKays seated themselves beside her. A strong medicinal smell rose up from the twins' bald tops.

"Food looks delicious, doesn't it?" Mrs. McKay said cheerily. "Now that we've gotten rid of those pesky lice, maybe we can work on fattening up the boys." The boys watched hungrily as she dished out chicken onto their plates.

Adrian doused his chicken with salt before Mrs. McKay had a chance to stop him. All of the boys ate ravenously in silence, as if they had not eaten in a week. Maybe they hadn't, thought Evelyn.

A pleasant surprise awaited them for dessert: ice cream. It was the first time any of them had eaten food so cold, sweet, and creamy. Everyone ate quickly, feeling as if they might miss their escorts if they lingered.

"I think Adrian may be ready to give up his salt tooth for an ice cream tooth," Mrs. McKay joked.

"Yes, well, if everyone has had their fill, maybe we ought to head back to the waiting area," Mrs. Thompson said. Nodding yes, everyone pulled their belongings from under the table, and moved back to the waiting benches.

The inspector pulled out some papers. "Is there a Mrs. McKay and three children here?" Gerald and Terry shot away from the bench without actually knowing what direction to run, but somehow they both landed into the arms of Mr. McKay who had just emerged from the dividing partition. Joyous laughter, hugging, tears. Evelyn had to look away. Jealousy ripped at her heart.

Mrs. McKay pulled the family back for one last goodbye. Mr. McKay chuckled at his bald twins, rubbing their heads with an open palm, saying he thought he might use their heads for a shaving mirror. Giggles abounding, the family took off.

Now it was just Maggie, Mrs. Thompson, and the Weir sisters. Again, the inspector shuffled some papers. Would it be Aunt Mabel?

The man looked up said, "There is a Mr. Thompson here looking for his wife and daughter." Disappointment coursed through Evelyn's veins.

"Oh, Da!" shouted Maggie, blonde braids airborne, as she crashed into her father's open arms. This was nearly more than Evelyn could take. She had to close her eyes to compose herself.

After a deep hug with her husband, Mrs. Thompson looked over her shoulder at the sisters. "Don't worry girls, we'll stay and wait with you until your aunt comes." The Thompsons sat politely next to the girls, but they could not contain their excited conversation with Mr. Thompson. The bench was buzzing with the electricity of their reunion. Maggie only had eyes for her father.

Evelyn sidled closer to Emily. Although she knew it was a ridiculous question, she couldn't help but ask Emily, "When will

Aunt Mabel get here?"

Emily smiled weakly, "In good time, I'm sure she'll be here. As Da says, 'Patience, my dear.'" Evelyn noticed Emily gripping the sides of her coat with white knuckles. Evelyn sat and waited, her foot nervously tapping.

Chapter 18
Mabel King

All Evelyn could do was wait and watch. Here in this smaller room, there wasn't much to see, but outside the door was a babbling brook of happy voices, and exclamations of joy in every language under the sun. Evelyn knew her meeting at the kissing post would not be this happy. Her memories of Aunt Mabel were hazy visions of coldness. She hoped her memories were wrong. As Lizzie might have said, think positively.

Emily pressed her elbow into Evelyn's side. "Evelyn, I think I see Aunt Mabel. See, over there with the gray hat." Emily nodded her head in a direction behind the inspector, through an opening door.

"Oh." Evelyn's stomach did a somersault. She saw a fifty-something-year-old woman walking across the threshold as if she were smelling something offensive.

"Is there an Emily and Winifred Weir present?" asked the inspector.

The girls stood and said, "Yes, sir." The Thompsons were so

deeply engaged in conversation, that Emily felt obliged to force a cough to alert them of their departure.

"Pardon me, Mrs. Thompson, but my aunt is here," said Emily.

"Of course! Let's go meet her!" Mrs. Thompson's jaunty tone was the polar opposite of the feeling of dread that had descended over Evelyn.

Evelyn suddenly remembered the similar feeling her stomach had while rolling down the grassy fields of Corbally. Stomach cartwheeling, feeling dizzy, she'd just let gravity take over.

Tentatively, Emily and Evelyn approached Aunt Mabel, who did not appear to recognize them.

Mabel King was dressed in expensive but dated clothes in tones of charcoal, her battleship gray hair pulled into an austere bun, topped by a drab hat. As the girls neared her, finally, a look of recognition spread across her hawkish face and she flashed a brisk smile. "Well, there you are, girls. You couldn't arrive soon enough! The crowds of foreigners are just dreadful, aren't they?"

A brief pressing together of shoulders served as a hug.

"Hello, Aunt Mabel, let me introduce you to Mrs. Thompson. She's been kind enough to wait with us." Emily spoke evenly and poised, although Evelyn noticed a slight quaver in her hand.

"Pleasure." Aunt Mabel offered a gloved hand and a limp handshake.

"Well, the girls will want to be off now, I'm sure. Wish you all the best, Emily and Evelyn." Mrs. Thompson enveloped Evelyn and Emily in a real mother's hug. Maggie bounced over to kiss Evelyn's cheek.

"Good luck in Stamford!" Maggie's crescent eyes twinkled and she skipped off with Mr. and Mrs. Thompson like bookends on either side.

"This way." Mabel King herded the girls to the exit door. She pointed to a queue for the ferry to Manhattan. Without offering to take their suitcases, she led them at a brisk pace up the ferryboat ramp.

Silently arranging their luggage at their feet, Emily and Evelyn waited for Aunt Mabel to speak.

"First, I must tell you that I prefer you call me 'Mrs. King' and not Aunty this or that. And next, please explain to me why Winifred is here instead of Anne. And why did that woman refer to Winifred as Evelyn?" Mrs. King glared at Emily through narrow, steel eyes.

"Yes, Aun . . . Mrs. King. Well, first, there was an unfortunate accident." As Emily told the story, Evelyn watched her aunt stiffen.

"I'll have you know that I was quite surprised to see Winifred's name on the ship master's list. I had to lie to the authorities to stop you from being deported for traveling under false pretenses. Now I suggest, Winifred, that you not speak to anyone about your true age or identity. You are to do as I say and we won't have any trouble." Mrs. King thrust out her pointy chin.

"Excuse me, Mrs. King, if you please, Winifred would prefer that you call her by her middle name, Evelyn . . . if you don't mind," said Emily, timidly looking up at Mrs. King.

Mrs. King glared at Evelyn as if to say that young girls should not have such strong opinions. "Well, I have to agree that Evelyn is far more adult sounding than Winnie. I'll have you know that I am completely disappointed not to have an older girl. Well, Evelyn, we'll just have to make do with you. You have some rather grown-up shoes to fill, don't you?"

Evelyn nodded, not knowing if Mrs. King was teasing as would Da, or if she meant to instill the fear of God in her. Without a doubt, Mrs. King had successfully achieved the latter.

Chapter 19
New York City Views

Mrs. King seemed intent on staring straight ahead in stony silence, so Evelyn glanced sideways at Emily, who was already looking out across the short distance of water to the New York City skyline. Evelyn turned to take in the view.

She craned her neck to see the top of a very tall building. She had read in one of Da's newspapers that the tallest skyscraper in New York City had been completed. It was called The Singer Building. Evelyn could not fathom how human hands had produced this gravity-defying structure. The up-down, jagged line of buildings made no sense to her. Everywhere she looked she saw concrete, metal, and other man-made materials. America seemed so artificial. Where was the color green? Would America be gray all over?

After the brief ferry ride across, Mrs. King muttered to the girls in exasperation, "Hurry!" They hauled their bags to another queue. This time, it appeared they were waiting for an electric streetcar. Without saying a word, Mrs. King dipped her gloved hand into her purse to gather the change for their fare and pointed to the steps of a waiting trolley.

Emily and Evelyn exchanged a brief look of incredulity at Mrs. King's peculiar way of communicating through pointing. Was this the American way? They boarded the streetcar and arranged their luggage at their feet, waiting for a cue from Mrs. King. After a few moments, however, it became clear that she was far more interested in glaring at the trolley driver's back. Evelyn turned to the window to scan a city view. On the street level, she was very disappointed to see smoky soot draping itself on everything. A rat scurried by, dodging carts, horses, and automobiles, at last disappearing into a hole under the curb. For a fleeting moment, Evelyn wished she could join that rat in his safe little home under this strange busy world.

A spicy smell blew into the trolley window as they passed a vendor selling sausages. A sign splashed with foreign words leaned against the cart. While a swarthy mustached man grilled foods, a line of people stood waiting to purchase his goods. Although she had eaten her fill, a feeling much like hunger gnawed at an empty spot in her belly.

The street scenes of New York were so complicated and disorderly. Fintona had one short street, with just a handful of two-story buildings, sharing identical roof lines. Here in New York, there was no symmetry, no order. A hodgepodge array of buildings, ranging from squalid to grand, in numbers she knew she could never count.

Evelyn thought back to her train ride through the city of Londonderry in Northern Ireland. Before New York, it had been the largest city she'd seen. Through a film of tears, she had viewed the scenes of Londonderry and noted tidy streets, snug shops and pubs lined up neatly against each other, chimneys lined up in straight rows. It was so tame compared to the wild chaos of New York City.

The shops of New York were stacked against each other, fighting for space, bursting with baskets and crates of goods, spilling right onto the sidewalk. Dirty-faced children stared at Evelyn's streetcar with hungry eyes. So this was the land of promise?

The streetcar took them to an enormous train depot called Grand Central Station. Evelyn, Emily, and Mrs. King entered a room even larger than the Great Hall at Ellis Island. Mouth agape, gazing up at the lofty ceiling, Evelyn marveled: America made everything so big! A gigantic cast iron eagle stared down from its perch high above on the decorative trim of the building. Evelyn felt a chill of recognition in the eagle's eye. Its intent glare was so similar to Mrs. King's bird-like eyes.

"This way," said Mrs. King, marching forward.

Evelyn read a sign above the train platform: New Haven Line. Another "new" thing in America, and yet the train seemed so dingy. Hanging onto Emily's warm hand, she plodded behind. The three boarded the train and settled onto worn, upholstered seats.

"All aboard!" shouted the conductor. He listed the train's stops, including Stamford. The doors shut with a thud, and the train lurched ahead. Evelyn shut her eyes as the train picked up speed. It was just like rolling down a hill, out of her control. She clasped Emily's hand and held on for dear life.

Part Three: Though the Wrong Seems Oft So Strong

Stamford, Connecticut, 1910–1919

Chapter 20
Miss Peartree
January 1910

Miss Peartree glanced at her watch. It was getting close to supper time and her canvas bag of sundries from King's Market seemed to grow in weight with every step. The sun was getting low in the sky, and a grim winter wind bit at her cheeks. Ominous clouds gathered, threatening yet another snow storm. Strands of her dark brown hair had slipped out from her hat and whipped at her eyes. As she rounded the corner of Franklin Street, she surveyed the brick row houses owned by her landlady. The entire block was the property of Mrs. King, who collected rent from the various buildings, and charged for room and board in her own house. Miss Peartree was currently a boarder in Mrs. King's house, along with several others. A cheerfully painted Victorian, with a whimsical carved balustrade on the front porch, the lighthearted feel of the house was the opposite of the all-business, no frills attitude of Mrs. King.

Nearing the house, Miss Peartree noticed a dim aura of a single gaslight glowing in the parlor window. Two girls were inside. Miss Peartree could see the silhouette of their bodies, bent over tiny lace work, the girls' faces intent on their handwork.

Poor dears, thought Miss Peartree. She worked as a teacher in the Franklin Street School and she was worried about these two Irish immigrants. They had not attended school since the day they arrived last October. Mrs. King seemed to demand far too much of them. Every time Miss Peartree was at the house, the girls were scrubbing floors, cooking meals for the boarders, and in any moment of spare time, straining their eyes over fine stitching. In addition to that, Emily had taken on the job of managing the accounts at the market. Too much for young girls, thought Miss Peartree.

As she crossed the threshold of the front door, the aroma of roasting lamb warmed her face. Those girls sure know how to cook, she thought. Since Mrs. King owned a meat market, the boarders were treated to a wholesome, if not top grade, cut of meat as their supper meal most evenings.

Miss Peartree was puzzled by Mrs. King. A brusque woman, she certainly was savvy when it came to making money. There was never mention of Mr. King, although Miss Peartree had noticed that now and then mail addressed to him would arrive at this house. Stiff formal handwriting on these envelopes redirected his mail to another address in Stamford. Certainly this was not a subject for discussion with Mrs. King. Miss Peartree shuddered, thinking of her landlady's severe disposition. She really did not want to upset Mrs. King. Miss Peartree felt fortunate to board at this house, so close to her job and shopping, not to mention the fine meals the girls served each night.

Walking up the stairs to her second floor room, she thought of the women who lived on this floor and shared the hall lavatory. Of course, Mrs. King occupied the grand front bedroom. Across the hall on either side of Miss Peartree's modest room were elderly boarders. There was Mrs. Krieger, who spent her days in a haze of confusion. When Miss Peartree had first moved in, she had tried to engage her in conversation. It had become quite clear in a matter of seconds that Mrs. Krieger did not dwell in the present. She did not seem aware of her surroundings, but would occasionally blurt out something in German. Miss Peartree had no idea if Mrs. Krieger had any relations. No one came to see her, except the daily visits from the Irish girls tending her needs. Then there was Mrs. Kowalski in the next room. Same vacant stare, only her infrequent mutterings came out in Polish.

On the first floor there was Mr. Santoriello, a recent immigrant from Italy who worked as a barber. He was hale and hearty, probably saving up his money to send for his family, buy a house, and maybe start his own business. Another man roomed in the backyard shed by the horse stables. Shady fellow, that Mr. Walker, thought Miss Peartree. So unkempt and smelling of alcohol. In the largest bedroom downstairs was Mrs. King's twenty-year-old son, Lester. Miss Peartree had half a mind to teach that impudent young man a lesson or two someday. So rude to everyone, especially when he was barking out demands to the two Irish girls. The only thing that held her tongue was the possibility of antagonizing Mrs. King. There was something very powerful about that woman.

An idea occurred to Miss Peartree. Stepping into the center hall, she quietly reached into her canvas bag and selected two plump oranges she had purchased at the market as a treat for herself. Within her bag, she also found two pretty ribbons she had bought for gift wrapping, but instead, with a straight pin, she attached a neat bow at the top of each orange. Next, in her careful teacher's cursive she jotted a note on brown grocery paper:

> *To the ladies of the house:*
> *Please join me for tea this Saturday at 4:00 PM.*
> *Your friend,*
> *Miss Peartree*

Miss Peartree slipped up the stairs to the girls' attic bedroom and left her gift in front of the door. She paused, remembering the murmur of sad voices and crying she had heard each night from this room during the months she had lived here. Shaking her head, she hoped she could brighten the girls' lives in some small way.

After a long day of educating the young minds of Stamford, Miss Peartree retreated to her room, ready to face a stack of papers to grade, but hoping for the interruption of the supper bell.

Chapter 21
Supper for Nine

Thump! Thump! Thump!

Evelyn and Emily startled, even though the noise was all too familiar. This was the sound of Mrs. King's wooden spoon pounding on the stove pipe in the kitchen. It was a message to the girls: You had better come swiftly to the kitchen to do your supper-time chores!

"Set down your needle, Evelyn," Emily said, jumping down from her chair.

"Oh, I just wanted to finish this row, so I won't lose my place when I pick it up again next time," said Evelyn. It was hard enough to make her lacework neat when she had full concentration. To put it down and pick it up made her work near impossible.

"Never mind your stitches, you know how Mrs. King gets when we don't come immediately," Emily said. Mrs. King had quickly established the law of the household. It was Evelyn and Emily's place to do as she commanded, never to hesitate, no less question. Of course, her own dear son, Lester, had a special place in the

house. Lester would be served hand and foot, never to lift a finger to help himself or others. Mrs. King had spoiled her son at the expense of everyone else in the house.

"Do hurry," Emily pleaded. Glancing down the hall for signs of Mrs. King, she reached for Evelyn's lace and said, "There, I've put it in just the right way for you to pick up again. I'll show you later how to keep better track of your stitches."

The two girls rushed to the kitchen where Mrs. King was impatiently tapping her foot, arms folded. "Now girls, the meat is just about cooked through and you have yet to make the gravy. Emily, you finish the cooking. Evelyn, you set the table. There will be five of us dining in the dining room. And prepare two trays for the invalids upstairs."

As Evelyn rushed to the dining room, Mrs. King shouted after her, "And don't forget to give Lester his special linens!"

Evelyn tossed a freshly pressed white linen across the polished table. Along the border of the cloth ran miniature embroidery over which Emily had labored for hours. The linen settled airily on the table. Next, Evelyn gathered the dishes the boarders were to use. They were not the finest, for those were relegated to special occasions, and one other exception. Lester was to have the best china for his place setting next to Mrs. King. It was quite ironic that Lester was lavished with such luxury. He certainly did not seem to appreciate it. Only last week Lester had broken his tea cup when he clumsily set it on the table with a thud. Evelyn had even wondered if he had done it on purpose. He seemed to enjoy the way Mrs. King fretted over Evelyn's job of picking up the shards, yet never once had she reprimanded Lester for having broken the cup in the first place. Evelyn just couldn't make sense of Mrs. King's behavior. She knew better than to speak up about the injustice. As Emily had reminded her, if she just bided her time, Da would come and make things right.

Dishes on the table, Evelyn rummaged in the drawer of a mahogany sideboard for cloth napkins. Lester had a special monogrammed set of linens. She neatly creased each cloth and angled one at every plate. Surveying the table, Evelyn felt rather proud of the handiwork she and Emily had contributed to this dining ensemble. At least the crisp white linens added some brightness to the otherwise dreary room. Mrs. King's house, while rich in possessions, seemed barren and dismal. So much dark wood, with fabrics in shades of maroon, gray, and dark green. In Corbally every room had whitewashed walls, reflecting what little light the small windows let in. Evelyn wondered if people could produce light. Her memory of home and family was drenched in light, except for the shadow cast on Ma's face. Here at Franklin Street, the grand-sized windows, gaslights, and electric bulbs somehow refused to illuminate.

In addition to the darkness of this house, it had taken some time for Evelyn to get used to eating meals the American way, the biggest meal of the day in the evening. No midday dinner, just a hurried small meal called "lunch." She realized how meals were so much more than simply eating food. Bowed heads and praying hands of Da, Ma, Emily, Annie, herself, and wee Tommy. Swapping tales, laughing, sharing.

"You are needed in the kitchen, Evelyn!" called Mrs. King. "The potatoes are absolute mush, you've boiled them so long."

The girls followed the brusque commands of Mrs. King. Emily whipped the potatoes and simmered the gravy. Mrs. King peered over their shoulders, making sure that they did not overindulge in ingredients or waste any of her food. The end result was a sumptuous, if not slightly overcooked, meal of lamb, mashed potatoes, gravy, and carrots. Assessing their labors, Mrs. King said, "This will do." She picked up the brass dinner bell, and marched to the center hall. With several waves of her wrist, she rang the bell, signaling the boarders to come to the dining room.

Miss Peartree and Mr. Santoriello exited their rooms and trotted through the hall to the dining room. Mr. Walker slipped in through the pantry door from the backyard. Lester was nowhere to be seen.

Mrs. King rang the bell again. Still no Lester.

"Oh that poor boy, he must be napping. Such a hard job he does for us down at the market, he must be exhausted." Mrs. King gathered her heavy skirt in her hands and bustled down the hall to Lester's bedroom door. Evelyn watched as Mrs. King's icy posture melted into slush. "Sweet Lester, please wake up! It's supper-time," she crooned to the closed door.

A loud bump and an irritated groan answered her back.

"The food is getting cold, honey, now please come," she urged in a syrupy voice.

With a low grunt, Lester emerged from his room looking puffy, one cheek chafed as if he had been lying upon it for some time.

"There you go, Lester, come see what the girls have cooked up for you tonight," Mrs. King said as she lovingly watched her son shuffle down the hallway.

As Lester lumbered ahead, the boarders waited in their places around the table, while Emily and Evelyn stood with trays of food. It seemed as if Lester took several extra minutes to move his chair back allowing room for his rather large girth. Finally, when Lester had assumed a sitting position, monogrammed napkin in lap, Mrs. King said, "Evelyn and Emily, please serve our boarders, but do see that Lester gets that tender piece of lamb. You know how he has digestive problems if the meat is too chewy."

Bracing herself against his bad manners, Evelyn stepped up to Lester with a large platter of lamb. She nervously forked a slice of meat and placed it on the center of the delicate white china plate. She dreaded dealing with Lester. She had never before met anyone so selfish and greedy.

"That's not enough!" barked Lester. Evelyn cringed and pierced another slice, laying it alongside its partner on Lester's plate. Lester snorted his satisfaction at the portion, and Evelyn moved along the table. Mrs. King sat rigid as Evelyn arranged some food on her plate. Mr. Walker's shadowy face watched as she placed meat on his plate. He smelled of the stable and something else she'd heard grown-ups call "the drink." She was relieved to serve the other boarders. Miss Peartree and Mr. Santoriello were far more polite and appreciative of the girls' service.

In a thick Italian accent, Mr. Santoriello said, "A delicious meal you have made for us, young ladies. Soon there will be a line of young men knocking at Mrs. King's door to ask for your hand in marriage." He wiped his black mustache with his napkin, looking pleased with himself. Mrs. King did not appear amused.

Miss Peartree broke the uncomfortable air with, "Emily and Evelyn are attractive young ladies, but it is their wit and kindness that are truly beautiful. As they say, 'Beautiful is as beautiful does.'" Miss Peartree was always armed with an arsenal of aphorisms. Evelyn enjoyed collecting her sayings and silently repeated the aphorism to memorize it.

Meanwhile, Lester had consumed his food in just a few gulps and requested more meat. Evelyn brought over the platter, which now held only a few meager slices. She and Emily would eat whatever the Kings and the boarders had not taken from the platter. Without waiting for Evelyn to serve him, Lester swiftly used his fork to rake the remaining meat onto his plate. He chewed loudly, grease drizzling out of the corner of his mouth. Evelyn watched in slight disgust as he used his delicate napkin to absorb the drips of gravy leaking from his mouth. She knew it would take an afternoon of laundering that napkin to get it back to its pristine condition.

"Emily and Evelyn, bring up the trays to our less fortunate boarders," Mrs. King said. Evelyn's heart dropped. Mrs. Krieger and Mrs. Kowalski relied on her help, but she couldn't help feeling revulsion at their physical state. They lay wasting in bed, looking like corpses. There was an odor of decay around them, and to make matters worse, it was Evelyn and Emily's job to empty fetid bedpans.

"Hurry now!" Mrs. King said, shaking her head in exasperation.

The girls hastened to the kitchen to fetch the two trays of food Emily had prepared earlier. Each plate had finely chopped meat and soft cooked vegetables, with a cup of tea sitting beside them. Balancing the trays, the girls worked their way through the hall and up the stairs.

When they had first arrived in Stamford, Evelyn could not bear to leave Emily's side, so the two would go into each of the ladies' rooms together. Unfortunately, this took up too much precious time, and Mrs. King had put a stop to this approach. Emily would service Mrs. Krieger, and Evelyn, Mrs. Kowalski.

Knocking first, but knowing that there'd be no reply, Evelyn always had a moment of panic. What if Mrs. Kowalski had died? She pushed the door open and still was not sure about Mrs. Kowalski's state. Then she detected the faint rising and falling of her chest beneath the blankets. Just as Emily had demonstrated, she used a cheerful loud voice to alert the woman of her presence.

"Good evening, Mrs. Kowalski." Evelyn set the tray down on the table beside the bed. "We've got some good food for you. It's time for you to sit up and eat." Although Evelyn could smell the bedpan, she had learned from experience that it did not pay to empty it until after supper.

Mrs. Kowalski's eyes opened and darted furtively from side to side, not comprehending her surroundings. Her thin white hair spread wildly in all directions across the pillow. "Clara?"

Evelyn had heard this name on previous visits. She answered, "It's Evelyn. Time for your supper."

Mrs. Kowalski looked at Evelyn and repeated, "Clara?" It wasn't worth the effort to contradict the woman, so Evelyn nodded and, as Emily had shown her, she gently raised Mrs. Kowalski from under her armpits and propped a pillow behind her back.

"There you go now. Are you comfortable?" Pulling a chair beside the bed, Evelyn began to spoon mashed potatoes into the crack of Mrs. Kowalski's mouth. Her face was a web of lines crisscrossing at angles across her features. Most of the potatoes dribbled down a crease in her chin. Evelyn dabbed a napkin to catch the mess. "Would you like some more, Mrs. Kowalski?" Evelyn tried a spoonful of carrots, followed by some tea. It was hard to tell if Mrs. Kowalski had consumed anything.

"Is there anything else you need?" She waited for a reply, but of course, Mrs. Kowalski was somewhere far away. "I'll add some coal to your stove and empty your bedpan." Evelyn poured out some more coal from the scuttle into the cast iron stove and prodded the embers with a poker. She turned back to tend to Mrs. Kowalski and the dreaded bedpan. Holding her breath, she reached for the pan and made a swift dash for the door to the hallway bathroom. Dumping the contents down the toilet, she forced herself to remember how she would like to be treated, should she ever become like Mrs. Kowalski. With dignity. But there still was something missing. No matter how hard she tried, she could not comprehend the loneliness of Mrs. Kowalski's life. Although Evelyn was heartbroken at her temporary separation from the rest of her family, she still had hope, and she still had Emily. Mrs. Kowalski had nothing. Evelyn rinsed the bedpan with tap water, and turning to the door, nearly collided with Emily and Mrs. Krieger's full bedpan.

"Oh, heaven help us, that would not be a pretty sight!" exclaimed Emily. Evelyn broke out in a relieved laugh and said, "I'm nearly done with Mrs. Kowalski. How about you?"

"Yes, and we'd better get back downstairs quickly. I am sure Mrs. King is ready for coffee."

Evelyn returned the bedpan to Mrs. Kowalski who seemed to have drifted back to sleep. Collecting the nearly untouched plate of food and tea, Evelyn took a glance around the room. Hanging from a mirror on the wall was a crucifix, and a small statue of the Virgin Mary. Evelyn recognized these as Roman Catholic holy relics similar to those she'd seen the few times she'd peeked through Hannah Curran's doorway in Corbally. Upon a bureau sat a sepia toned photograph of a serious faced couple. Wearing clothes from another era and another country, Evelyn had assumed this was Mr. and Mrs. Kowalski at a happier and healthier time of her life. What had become of Mr. Kowalski? And who was Clara? Surely there was a tale to be told here.

Evelyn met Emily in the hall, set down the trays, and followed her back to the bathroom to wash away any traces of the invalids. Picking up the barely touched dinners, they hurried down the last flight of stairs, and saw the top of Mrs. King's bun. She was waiting for them at the bottom step.

"What took you two so long? How many times do I have to tell you girls not to dawdle? Come, now, Emily, get the coffee brewing and Evelyn, you clear the table."

Evelyn dipped in-between each diner and collected the plates and silverware. Carrying a tall stack to the kitchen sink, Emily passed her with a pot of coffee. "Could you bring in the cream?"

"I'll be right back with it." Evelyn and Emily had worked out a system for cooking, serving, and cleaning that was very efficient, even if Mrs. King thought otherwise.

Coffee served, Emily and Evelyn finally had a moment to sit

down at the small kitchen table alone to eat their supper.

"Ah, what a feast we shall have. A shred of lamb. A lump of cold potatoes. A delightfully squashed carrot!" joked Emily.

"If you drown it all in gravy, it actually tastes quite good," said Evelyn, pouring some steaming gravy directly from a pan on the stove.

These moments together by the glow of the warm kitchen stove were restorative for the girls. They giggled over Mr. Santoriello's compliment, and imagined Mrs. King's reaction to a suitor taking away her Bridgets.

"She'd scare them all away with her wooden spoon," whispered Emily. The girls laughed in hushed tones, glancing over their shoulder for signs of Mrs. King. Soon she would be calling them to clear away the coffee cups.

"Evelyn, you can start the dishes in the sink and I'll clear the coffee cups from the table." Emily knew that Evelyn still preferred washing dishes, especially now with the magic of indoor running water and the wonderful soapy bubbles that Americans used for washing.

As Evelyn scrubbed each plate, she no longer had fantasies about fairies. Now her head was dancing with visions of real human faces. Maggie Thompson and her storybook perfect family. Capable Lizzie Askin triumphing in her new life in Brooklyn, New York. The funny little McKay boys wrestling like puppies on the floor of their new home in Philadelphia. Puppies . . . what had become of sweet Linwood? Then there were those dear faces from home, so far across a vast ocean.

Chapter 22
Some Light in the Dark

Later that night, with aching feet, Evelyn and Emily made their way up to the third flight of stairs to their bedroom. Dishes washed, dried, and stored on shelves, they had checked on each of the potbellied stoves in the boarders' rooms, loading them with enough coal to burn through the night. Making a stop in the second floor bathroom, shared by the women of the house, they washed away the soot from tending the stoves. Through the window of the hall, Evelyn noticed that it was snowing. Again. Snow in Stamford accumulated in volumes that Evelyn had never seen before. Back in Corbally, on the rare occasion of a snow shower, it would melt away as soon as it touched the green grass. Here in Stamford there was no time to go outside and play in the wondrous deep snow.

As they reached the top step, in the dim gaslight glow they noticed two small orbs cheerfully reflecting orange light.

"What on earth is that?" asked Emily.

"Oh, Em, look, I believe they are oranges!" Evelyn declared. She recognized the tropical fruit from King's Market. It certainly was a treat to have fruit shipped from so far away in the middle of the winter.

"You're right, Evelyn. And look, there's a note." Emily lifted the brown paper under the light. "It's from Miss Peartree, and she wants us to join her for tea tomorrow."

Suddenly the girls' weariness lifted. Stepping into their cramped room, Emily tossed the oranges onto the bed they shared. The ribbons fell off, and the oranges rolled to a stop at a pillow's edge. Emily tied a ribbon back on, but this time she wrapped it around the north and south pole, knotting the top and said, "If I don't say so myself, doesn't this orange bear a strong resemblance to Mr. Turnball suffering from a toothache?"

At that, Evelyn burst into a cascade of giggles. Mr. Turnball was a nearly bald and round middle aged bachelor who frequented King's Market. He had a habit of flirting with Emily, demanding her attention away from the columns of figures she needed to calculate as she did the accounting for Mrs. King. It hadn't taken long for Mrs. King to discover Emily's talent in arithmetic, and she had quickly seized the opportunity to save money on a hired bookkeeper and used her niece's free labor instead.

"Let me have Mr. Turnball, Em," said Evelyn. With a quick toss, Mr. Turnball flew through the air and landed in Evelyn's open palm.

"That couldn't have helped the pain of your old toothache, poor fellow," said Emily.

Evelyn dug her fingernail into the orange skin and carved out two droopy eyes and a scowl. "There, now we really have a close resemblance!"

"It's off to the dentist with you, Mr. Turnball," said Emily.

"I've seen some toothaches in my day, but I'm afraid I've never seen one this size! It'll have to be removed." Evelyn mimicked the low voice of a dentist.

"Will there be any pain?" asked Mr. Turnball, as played by Emily.

"Ah, yes, there will be a lot of pain. Now just sit still while I get my extracting tools." Evelyn pretended to sharpen her fingernails with a file. With a devilish grin, she dug into the orange's mouth and shaped a jack-o'lantern grin.

"Ay, the pain," moaned Emily, her giggles breaking through the drama.

"What a handsome fellow you have become. Maybe that lovely British girl down at King's Market will take a shine to you now," said Evelyn. The girls fell onto the bed in free-flowing laughter.

In the bedroom below, Miss Peartree took a moment from her school papers to listen. She smiled. At long last, the girls were laughing!

Chapter 23
A Day's Labor

"Time to wake up, Evelyn!" Emily said, pulling back the covers from Evelyn's side of the bed. The third floor room was drafty, and the frosty Connecticut temperatures were impossible to get used to. Through the tiny window of their attic bedroom, she viewed snow crusted tree branches. Evelyn could see her breath as she sighed. Last night's fun had faded into the reality of another day of work in Stamford without her whole family.

"Em . . . I was wondering . . . when will Ma and Da come with the family?" Evelyn pulled the blankets to her chin and waited for a reply.

"It's not likely to be soon. From Ma's letters, times have been hard. The cattle are falling sick, one by one, and the weather has been so wet, the hay hasn't had a chance to dry properly. And, of course, the baby's due to come any day."

"I know, but Da promised." Evelyn's voice cracked. She had an ache in the pit of her belly.

"Give them time, Evelyn." Emily set down a hair brush and took Evelyn's two hands into hers. "You are a Weir, Evelyn.

Make your family proud. Lord knows it's hard, but you must be patient."

"Emily, do you ever get sad?" Evelyn asked.

"Of course, I do! Haven't you caught me sniffling my way through one of Ma's letters?" Emily sidled closer to Evelyn, her face serious. "And you know, there is something else that bothers me. In fact, I feel angry a lot. Angry at how Mrs. King treats us. As if we were beneath her, and here we are, her own family."

Evelyn angled her head. She had rarely seen Emily so indignant. "But what can we do about it?"

Emily threw her arms up and answered, "That's just it! We can't speak out against her. Wouldn't be respectful. She's paid our way, she feeds us, provides our room. But most of all, she's Da's sister. Da mustn't know how awful she and Lester are. We need to keep our letters to Ma and Da positive. We can manage this, Evelyn. And it will all get better when the family joins us."

"Emily, sometimes I just don't know how I can get through." Evelyn swallowed hard, tears glistening on her lashes.

"Yes, yes, I know that feeling. But when I start feeling heartbroken, I think about an important job I have, and that takes my mind off my troubles."

"What job? Do you mean all the nasty chores Mrs. King gives us?" Evelyn sat up in bed, resting her chin against her bent knees, staring intently at Emily.

"No, Evelyn. Taking care of you! That's what keeps me going." Emily smiled and looked deep into Evelyn's eyes. "You've got to tell yourself each and every day that things will get better. And know that we'll always have each other." Emily patted Evelyn's back. "There, now, it certainly could be a lot worse. Look at poor old Mrs. Krieger and Mrs. Kowalski. Now those two certainly have a sad story."

Evelyn thought about this as she wiggled into a work dress, pulling it over her long underwear. Mrs. King had seen to it that the girls had plenty of store-bought dresses from the five and dime store. But they never seemed to fit the way Ma's homemade pinafores did. Evelyn asked, "Emily, what happened to Mrs. Kowalski's family?"

"Don't know. Neither Mrs. Kowalski nor Mrs. Krieger could tell you if you asked, anyway. Lost their minds, poor things." Emily finished tying the end of a single braid down her back.

Putting her arm around Evelyn, she said, "Come, now, time to get breakfast cooking."

Thump! Thump! Thump!

Emily and Evelyn picked up speed through the halls and down the stairs to the opposite end of the house where the kitchen was located. Mrs. King stood at the doorway, waiting.

"Late again!" she said, pivoting towards the kitchen. The girls swapped a quick look and followed.

Preparing breakfast was so automatic for the girls that they each went to their tasks silently. Evelyn had grown used to moving through the Franklin Street house with a hollow carved out of her insides. She was resigned to let gravity pull her through each moment, each task, each day.

She filled a large kettle with tap water while Emily struck a match to light a stovetop burner.

Next, she went to the pantry to fetch the porridge and sugar. Evelyn had to admit, this pantry was a wonderland of food. There were more boxes, jars, and cans of food here on the shelves than Da had ever stocked in his entire shop at Clabby. She scooped porridge from a tin in the pantry, and reached for a sack of sugar. Emily had warmed some milk, cold from the ice box. Tea bags placed at the bottom of the teapot, and coffee ground in a mill, Evelyn pulled out some store bought slices of bread from a bag for toast. Water boiling, porridge simmering, bread toasting, the table still needed to be set. Mrs. King watched with hawk eyes as the girls hurried through the kitchen. "Stir the oatmeal, Emily. It's starting to stick," she said.

Evelyn scooted out to the dining room to lay out the dishes. Through the window, she caught a view of the sun rising behind snow-laced tree branches. Mr. Walker had shoveled a path from the stables to the front of the house. The purple sky was reflected in a frozen puddle. How Tommy would love to smash that ice with a stone.

Mr. Walker was the first to arrive at the table, looking unwashed and unshaven, snow sprinkled on the tip of his purple nose. In his husky voice he said a curt, "Good morning," to the girls, lowering his mouth to the steaming cup of coffee Emily had served him.

Mr. Walker tended the stables and four horses. In addition to the income Mrs. King gathered from the boarders, she collected money for allowing other people the use of the horse stables behind the house. Every inch of her property seemed to be put to use for making a profit. Mr. Walker also worked as a delivery man for Mrs. King, moving goods from market to market, and delivering food to wealthy customers in nearby Greenwich.

Miss Peartree hurried in, pulling a shawl around her shoulders. "Chilly morning! At least my room was toasty warm thanks to the delightful fire you girls had going in the bedroom stove." Miss Peartree smiled primly and added, "So, will I be seeing you girls later?"

Evelyn thought she saw Mrs. King bristle at Miss Peartree's friendly overtures. "Yes, we'd love to, Miss Peartree." Glancing at Mrs. King across the room, Emily added, "Of course, we'll have to finish all of the house chores first. But since today is Saturday, I won't be going into the market." Monday through Friday, Emily was expected to work in the market.

"That would be just lovely," Miss Peartree replied, seating herself across from Mr. Walker.

Mr. Santoriello walked into the room, buttoning up his vest. "Good morning to you!" He gave a slight bow in the direction of Mrs. King and the girls, and sat beside Miss Peartree.

"Smells like American coffee. Good enough, but I have to admit, I miss the espresso of my home. You need to drink four cups of this coffee to get the same effect." He chuckled as Emily poured coffee into his cup. With his olive skin, slick pomaded black hair, and dense accent, he hardly resembled Da. Yet there was something in his demeanor that reminded Evelyn of her father.

"Evelyn, get the oatmeal. We are not waiting for Lester this morning. He was out late, and he needs his sleep," Mrs. King said, sitting down at the head of the table. Emily and Evelyn were well aware of Lester's late return. He and his boisterous friends had been out carousing, making a racket as Lester stomped into the house a few hours before dawn. Evelyn was beginning to suspect that Lester had a penchant for drinking, just like Mr. Walker.

Emily joined Evelyn in the kitchen, buttering the toast and piling it onto a platter. They tracked back into the dining room serve the waiting boarders. Evelyn thought how in a few months' time, she and Emily had certainly worn a path in the wooden planks between the kitchen and dining room.

"Lovely breakfast, girls. Thank you so much," Miss Peartree said as the girls dished out the oatmeal and offered the toast.

Breakfast was a quick meal, as Mr. Santoriello and Mr. Walker were both in a hurry to get to work. As they excused themselves from the table, Evelyn and Emily cleared the dishes.

"I'd love to sit here and while away this Saturday morning, but 'Lost time is never found again.' I'm afraid it's time for me to face my students' arithmetic examinations," Miss Peartree said. Neatly setting her spoon alongside her bowl, she sipped the last drop of her coffee. Peering from under her spectacles, she said to the girls, "I am looking forward to seeing you later." She rose and headed up the stairs to her room.

Mrs. King looked at the girls skeptically and said, "I must be off to the market, and I am trusting you girls to take care of everything. There'll be no lingering and socializing. You are not to speak with anyone who might come to the house, Evelyn. Remember what I have told you about the authorities." Reaching into her purse, she turned to Emily, "We are running low on ice, so please put the ice sign in the front window. Here is some money to pay the iceman." Mrs. King held out a paper bill and some coins. "Today is Saturday, and that means laundering the bed sheets of our two invalids. In addition, every room must be swept, every stove emptied of ashes." Mrs. King narrowed her eyes at the girls and added. "Every room, that is, except Lester's. You are not to disturb him." Pulling back her shoulders and straightening her back, she stepped deliberately to the front door where she plucked a hat from a rack. Pulling it on, she grimaced into the dark mirror, then gathered her purse and a canvas shopping bag, and exited through the front door.

With a sigh of relief, Emily turned to Evelyn and said, "Come now, I am absolutely famished. Let's have some breakfast."

Evelyn's mood brightened as Mrs. King vanished out of sight. Today the girls would be free of her stern scrutiny and best of all, guests at a tea party. No matter that there were so many chores, she'd have Emily's company all day. Perhaps the hardest thing she had to deal with in Stamford was the time she spent running errands and cleaning the house while Emily worked at the market.

With feet as light as they'd ever been in this house, Evelyn skipped to the kitchen table where Emily was pouring the tea. Evelyn gave her oatmeal an extra flourish of brown sugar, now that Mrs. King was not there to ration her supplies. Crunching on some toast, she said, "Emily, let's try to finish our chores early, so we can have plenty of time with Miss Peartree."

"Absolutely! I think we should start with the bedsheets. They'll have a chance to dry while we sweep out the rest of the rooms."

Chores with Emily passed quickly. They fed Mrs. Krieger and Mrs. Kowalski and then moved them into wheelchairs.

"Let's roll them to the window, Em. Maybe the ladies would enjoy a view," Evelyn said. From the second floor window the ladies could see the Episcopal Church and its graveyard. Pushing the chair into place, Evelyn added, "On second thought, it's not the most optimistic view, now is it?" She shared a short laugh with Emily and suddenly noticed something white in Mrs. Kowalski clutched fist. Later, thought Evelyn, when she and Emily gave her a sponge bath, she'd see what it was.

They brought the used sheets down to the laundry sink, soaked them in bleach, scrubbed them against a washboard and squeezed them through a wringer. It was too cold to dry them outdoors, so the girls hung them on a clothes line strung in front of the kitchen stove.

Sweeping each room and emptying ashes from stoves, the girls coughed from the dust and soot. Stopping in to clean Miss Peartree's room, they enjoyed a brief conversation and a preview of what was to come later.

"I have some books to share with you girls. And I'd love to tell you about the women's club I belong to, all the causes we work for. But I don't want to keep you from your work. And please don't worry about fixing me lunch today. I've got some crackers and an apple to munch on. Of course, we'll enjoy some sweets with tea at four o'clock. We'll talk later!" Miss Peartree sat at an open roll top desk, dipping the nib of her pen into ink, marking each student's paper.

Breaking for a brief lunch, the girls heard the bell of the iceman's horse and cart stopping in front. Emily directed him to the kitchen icebox where he unloaded the fresh ice and she paid him.

The clean dry sheets back on the beds, Evelyn and Emily gathered some soap and sponges to bathe the two old ladies. Wheeling them into the bathroom, this job was done as quickly as possible, so as not to expose them to the cold. Mrs. Kowalski did not like being touched, and the girls swabbed hastily, uttering reassuring words.

As Evelyn unfolded Mrs. Kowalski's fist to wash her hands, she noticed that the white thing in her hands was gone. Maybe she had just imagined it.

Mrs. Krieger offered less resistance, her paper thin skin sagging from her fragile bones. She slumped over, and the girls had to prop her up with one hand, dabbing with the other, to keep her from falling out of her wheelchair. Evelyn thought how there was such a fine line between Mrs. Krieger's life and death: one shallow breath away.

Next, with the two ladies tucked safely in their beds, Emily paused to think. "Let's see; we've laundered the bed sheets, swept out the bedrooms and the stoves, paid the ice man . . . is there anything else?"

"Since we still have a half hour before tea, why don't we peel the potatoes for tonight's supper? Less preparation later," Evelyn said.

"There you are! You are starting to think like a true Weir." As the girls headed downstairs, they heard the creak of Lester's bedroom door opening, followed by a slam as it closed. They stopped in their tracks as they heard him pace to the front door. A draft of cold air surged up the stairs as he opened the door and left.

"Another bit of good luck for us today. No more Lester," Emily whispered as they continued down to the kitchen.

Peeling potatoes at the countertop, Evelyn looked up at a calendar hanging above the sink. It was decorated with an advertisement for Yale & Towne Manufacturing Co. Located on Pacific Street, the company had an enormous complex of buildings that dominated Stamford's industry. Many of the customers who shopped at King's Market, also located on Pacific Street, were employed by Yale & Towne, a manufacturer of locks and keys. Evelyn looked at today's date: January 28, 1910. Why, it was Emily's seventeenth birthday! How could she make this a special day for her sister?

Across the kitchen, setting a heavy pot of water onto the stovetop, Emily seemed lost in thought. An idea bloomed in Evelyn's mind.

Chapter 24
Tea for Three

It was nearly four o'clock. The girls had washed up and put on their best work dresses. Emily had carefully brushed out Evelyn's hair until it shone like silk. Tucked under her armpit, Evelyn clutched a small package.

"What have you got there?" Emily asked.

"You'll have to wait and see later," Evelyn answered, smiling mysteriously.

"All right . . . let's hurry and make the tea." Emily led the way to the kitchen, with Evelyn stopping in the dining room to pull down three teacups and saucers from the cupboard. Back in the kitchen, she filled a creamer and stuck a spoon into a sugar bowl filled to the brim. The abundance of food here in Aunt Mabel's kitchen still amazed her.

When the water had come to a boil, Emily filled a teapot and arranged the dishes on a tray.

"Tea's ready!" Emily said, lifting the tea service and heading to the second floor. Evelyn followed, her secret package stowed in her apron pocket.

Evelyn knew time would be short. Mrs. King would surely be back by five to supervise supper preparations. One hour of sipping tea, eating sweets, and chatting among friends. Almost like home!

They knocked on Miss Peartree's door and heard her call, "Coming, girls!"

The sound of light footsteps approached the door, and Miss

Peartree's smiling face appeared. "Come on in, my dears." She extended her arm and pointed to three chairs arranged in a circle around a small round table. A vase holding a single yellow jonquil stood at the center. A platter of golden brown pastries sat beside it. Evelyn's mouth watered as she noticed red jam leaking out of the sides of several. Emily set down the tray on the table.

Propped against the wall behind the circle of chairs were some banners. Courage. Wisdom. Unselfishness. Apparently Miss Peartree had been stitching these banners for her club. Evelyn knew that there'd certainly be an explanation.

"Take a seat, and let's have our tea before it gets cold," Miss Peartree said, reaching for a stack of books and papers.

Emily poured tea into each cup and looked up expectantly at her hostess.

"Well, now, you've surely noticed the banners I've made." Miss Peartree stretched her arm towards the flags. "I pulled them out for you to admire." She dipped a level spoon of sugar into her cup, added a dash of cream, and stirred.

"The women's club I belong to is very active in advocating the right for women to vote. We call it 'women's suffrage.' Why, we are in the process of planning a march down Fifth Avenue in New York City next May. Did you notice the yellow flower here? It's our symbol for the cause. Quite disappointing that the federal government has not given women the right to vote yet. But I have a lot of hope that it will happen soon." She paused to take a sip of tea. Holding up the platter of pastries, she asked, "A sweet, Evelyn?"

Evelyn took a miniature turnover that hinted at jam buried within. Emily helped herself to a similar pastry, and Miss Peartree continued.

"My club meets once a week at the Ferguson Library meeting room. We discuss current events and issues regarding the improvement of life for women, children, and the underprivileged." She paused to take a sip of tea. "I have been watching you girls, and I have noticed how hard you work. Your diligence is a good character trait. I can also see your intelligence. Do you think there's any chance that Evelyn will be allowed to attend school?"

Evelyn darted a look at Emily, who nodded in encouragement for Evelyn to speak. Evelyn said, "Well, you see, Miss Peartree,

Mrs. King says that the authorities mustn't know that I'm here in America. My sister, Annie, was supposed to come, but when she broke her leg, I had to take her place."

Evelyn swallowed as Miss Peartree listened intently, watching over lowered glasses.

"Mrs. King says my papers are not legal. She says when she met us at Ellis Island she had to lie and pretend I was Annie to get admitted. So, if I were to enroll in school, the authorities would find out and deport me."

Miss Peartree clucked. "Doesn't sound right to me. No, not at all!" Pushing her glasses against her face, she said, "Well, Mrs. King is not one to cross. And I would like to help further your education here at the house."

The girls exchanged a quick look.

"I will have books available for you, and we can meet each week to discuss their contents. A book club, you might call it." Miss Peartree bit into a pastry and chewed thoughtfully. Wiping the sides of her mouth with a napkin, she asked, "What do you think?"

"Sounds too good to be true. But how will Mrs. King feel about it?" Emily asked.

"With all due respect, she never has to find out. Mrs. King has her reasons for being the way she is." Miss Peartree turned to her stack of books.

"But what if we can't keep up with all the reading? It's been so long since I've had a book to read or attended school," Evelyn said with a worried face.

"Dear Evelyn, 'Our greatest glory is not in never falling, but in rising every time we fall.'" Miss Peartree pulled some books onto her lap.

"How do you know so much, Miss Peartree?" Evelyn asked, leaning out of her chair.

"Reading, reading, and more reading. I just quoted the great Chinese philosopher, Confucius. We can learn so much by listening to others who have come before us. 'We have two ears and one mouth so that we can listen twice as much as we speak.' And that quote was from the ancient Epictetus." She laughed lightly. "I have my own version: We have two eyes and one mouth so that we can read twice as much as we speak."

Emily and Evelyn watched Miss Peartree in amazement.

"Now, to get started, I've got a useful book for you, Evelyn: *The*

American Girl's Handy Book, by Dan Beard and his sisters. It is chock-full of ideas for making useful and playful items, as well as instructions for practical living."

"Thank you, Miss Peartree!" Evelyn took the book gingerly and, brushing her hand across the cover, she inhaled the smell of ink and paper.

"As for you, Emily, another useful book for more adult pursuits: *Hill's Manual of Social and Business Forms, Twentieth Century Edition*." Miss Peartree handed Emily the book. "You'll notice how this book covers everything from basic penmanship to the structure of the government of our country. A handbook for living in this new century!"

"We just don't know how to thank you, Miss Peartree," Emily said, tucking the thick tome onto her lap.

"Emily and Evelyn, with all the work you do for me, surely it is I who needs to say the thank you." Miss Peartree tipped her cup to her mouth. "And don't forget, we'll meet every Saturday, same time. Four o'clock."

Evelyn and Emily finished eating their pastries and gulped down the last of the tea.

Miss Peartree said, "I almost forgot! Here are some writing tablets for you to jot down thoughts about your reading, or anything at all on your mind."

Taking a tablet, Evelyn suddenly remembered her surprise. "Thank you so much, Miss Peartree. But there's one more thing. I'd like to honor Emily today with a very small present. After all, it's not every day that your sister turns seventeen." Evelyn, feeling slightly self-conscious, but determined to make her sister's day special, pulled out the package from her pocket.

"Well, well, Emily, congratulations! A birthday today!" Miss Peartree rested a hand on Emily's back, and with her other hand, pulled the jonquil out of the vase. "Had I known, I'd have purchased a rose for the occasion." She handed Emily the flower.

"Oh, that's not necessary," Emily blushed, taking the flower into her hands.

"A rose? Don't worry, Miss Peartree, I've taken care of it. Here's a very special kind of rose for you, Emily." Evelyn handed Emily the package.

Emily opened it, not sure of what her sister meant.

Evelyn added, "It may not look like much at this point, but it may carry some meaning for you. I know it means something to me . . ." Evelyn watched as Emily untied a ribbon and opened a matchbox. Inside were scattered rose petals, dried and brittle.

"Evelyn! The rose from Da! The day we left on the train . . ." Emily's eyes brimmed with tears.

Miss Peartree watched as Emily hugged Evelyn. "There, there, Emily. We all need a good cry now and then. 'Sorrow concealed, like an oven stopp'd. Doth burn the heart to cinders where it is.' That's Shakespeare."

After a moment's silence, the sound of the front door opening made the girls stiffen. They listened for the footsteps of Mrs. King, but the heavy tread that followed surely belonged to Lester. His bedroom door slammed with extra force.

"Oh, dear, if Lester's home, Mrs. King must be close behind." Emily stood, brushing her hand across her moist eyes. She arranged the dishes upon the tray and piled the books and tablets.

"It's best you hurry off now." Miss Peartree stood and helped stack the dishes onto the tray. "I'll see you at supper, now that we've thoroughly spoiled our appetites!"

Emily went downstairs, and Evelyn went upstairs to drop off the books and the birthday flowers. She took a quick peek at the pages within her book, but knew she'd better hurry to her place in the kitchen. Resuming their places at the kitchen sink, the girls washed and dried the dishes they'd used. Since Mrs. King had not returned, they went to the parlor to continue their lacework until she arrived with this evening's supper ingredients.

"Do you see where you need to begin your next stitch?" Emily asked.

"Yes, now I see how to do it. But I don't think I'll ever be as good as you, Em."

"Of course you will. You just need to be seventeen years old, just like me!"

The front door rattled and Mrs. King stepped inside. Without wasting a moment, she called from the vestibule, "Girls! Come get my bags. Time to cook supper."

This time Evelyn knew how to set down her lace without losing her place. She and Emily met Mrs. King at the door.

Mrs. King said impatiently, "I hope you're done with more lace. We've sold out all of our stock and customers want more."

Emily lifted a bag in each hand and Evelyn took the remaining one. "We're nearly done with our next pieces, Mrs. King," Emily said.

"Well, I certainly hope so." Mrs. King hung her hat on a hook. "There's German sausage in your bag, Evelyn. I'll have to show you how to cook it for dinner." Turning to Emily, she added, "In your bag, Emily, there's some Philip's Milk of Magnesia. It's a special tonic made here in Stamford. Bring some up to poor Lester. He's having a bad time with his stomach today." Emily gave Evelyn a knowing look behind Mrs. King's back, and rushed up the stairs to deliver the medicine to Lester.

This night was like so many others: cooking, serving, cleaning under the watchful eyes of Mrs. King. Later, at the small kitchen table with Emily, Evelyn enjoyed the unusual new taste of the German sausage: salty and spicy. She felt warm inside; the hollow had filled up temporarily with good food and hope. Nothing Mrs. King or Lester said or did could bring Evelyn down from her high spirits. Today had been a good day in Stamford. She had a book to read and she had made a real friend in Miss Peartree.

Chapter 25
Sunday in Stamford

During the long winter nights, bedtime was especially difficult for Evelyn. Nightly prayers for her family made her dizzy with homesickness. Making matters worse, she couldn't help herself from rereading the few letters from Ma over and over, with the hope of discovering news of an imminent reunion secretly embedded within. But the letters only told the same story of bad crops, sick cattle, and a long, hard pregnancy. Annie was well, keeping very busy with all of the chores and watching Tommy, who had recently turned three years old. Ma spent her days resting in bed, as ordered by Doctor Fulton, waiting for the baby to arrive in the late winter. Da spent all daylight hours in the fields that yielded so little food.

Lizzie had sent word of her new position in Brooklyn. She and Sarah "were taking the city by storm." They had plans to save their earnings and open their own business, a bookshop. How Evelyn wished she had reason to share the same enthusiasm for her position at Franklin Street.

Miss Peartree's books were a welcome distraction, but because Mrs. King demanded so much lace, the girls needed most of their spare time for that pursuit. During the month of February, Evelyn had managed to read the book *Heidi,* which she adored. Emily was slowly working her way through *Jane Eyre,* but she was even more burdened with lace orders, taking on half of Evelyn's as well.

Sunday was Evelyn's favorite day of the week. It was a respite from the routine drudge of cooking, cleaning, tending boarders, and lace-making. Neither Lester nor Mrs. King attended church regularly, but the girls were allowed time each Sunday to worship across the street at the Episcopal Church.

One March Sunday morning after breakfast chores and tending Mrs. Kowalski, Evelyn got dressed in her church clothes. Donning a gauzy white dress from The Martin Brother's Store, Evelyn smoothed the gossamer fabric and thought about the day when Mrs. King had taken her shopping. Mrs. King had asked a saleslady to snatch up as many dresses in Evelyn's numbered size. Evelyn had hastily pulled them on. Mrs. King had barely examined the fit or quality, nodding to the clerk to tally the cost. Evelyn was intrigued by the idea that it would actually be profitable for a company to produce masses of clothing of various sizes ahead of time, and then count on enough people purchasing them to cover the expense of making so many of them. The motto of Martin's store was, "We aim to please and clothe the masses at the lowest cost." It seemed wasteful to make so many extra dresses, just in case someone might fit them. So different from Mrs. Mulhern's dress shop in Fintona, where each dress was custom designed and fitted to a single body. Apparently the idea of mass production worked. Stamford certainly provided proof, with the proliferation of factories, shops, and elegant houses of wealthy residents on Broad Street.

Parting her hair down the center with a comb, Evelyn thought about the new acquaintances she'd made at church. Mrs. King had an older son, Ralph, who lived in one of the row houses on Franklin Street with his wife and three-year-old daughter, Doris. This family attended the same church, and while Evelyn did not feel much friendliness from Ralph and his wife, she couldn't help but enjoy the attentions of Doris. Doris had chosen Evelyn as her favorite companion at church, waddling behind her like a duckling.

"I don't know what you've done to get Doris's affections, Evelyn. Have you plied her with sweets?" Emily had joked.

Evelyn wasn't sure why Doris had selected her, except she knew that the feeling was mutual. Doris was a breath of fresh air, whisking away the stale sad atmosphere of 89 Franklin Street.

"Are you ready, Em?" Evelyn asked, as she fastened the last

button of her Sunday dress.

"Yes, I'm ready." Evelyn looked up to see Emily wearing a similar white dress, sporting a new hairstyle. She had swept her hair up high into a Gibson-girl bun, much like the advertisements in *The Ladies Home Journal.* No longer girlish, Evelyn realized, Emily could easily be mistaken for a full grown woman.

"You look pretty, Em," Evelyn said.

"And so do you, my dear!" Smiling, Emily gathered a crocheted shawl from her closet, and headed for the door.

As the girls made their way down the third floor stairs, a faint sound came from below, in Mrs. Kowalski's room. It sounded like an object sliding across the wooden floor. Then, silence.

Emily and Evelyn swapped a wide-eyed look. "We'd better look in on Mrs. Kowalski," Emily said.

Evelyn's heart beat fast, worried about what she might find.

Knocking first, but hearing no response as usual, Emily eased the door open.

Before them, Mrs. Kowalski lay in bed, her bird-like body eclipsed by the grand spool bed, with its four tall spires. Her eyes gazed vacantly sideways and there was a slight smudge of pink on each cheek. She was breathing heavily, as if she had been exerting herself.

"Is everything all right, Mrs. Kowalski?" Emily asked, stepping closer.

A barely audible groan came from the crack of her mouth. Emily looked over her shoulder at Evelyn and shrugged.

Evelyn scanned the room for anything unusual. The holy relics were all in place, and the furniture tidy and gleaming, thanks to the careful polishing the girls gave it each week. Beneath the spool bed was an old trunk. On second glance, Evelyn thought it looked slightly crooked. She bent down to straighten it.

"Everything seems in order," Emily said.

"Have a good rest, Mrs. Kowalski, and we'll be back at lunchtime," Emily said, patting Mrs. Kowalski's arm. They left, gently closing the door behind.

"Do you think Mrs. Kowalski is more aware than she lets on? I mean, do you think she can get out of bed and move around?" Evelyn asked Emily as they arrived on the bottom step.

"Oh, it certainly doesn't seem possible. She's as weak as a newborn kitten. And it's clear her mind is gone."

"I know she seems that way, but sometimes, I wonder . . ." Evelyn set aside the thought and continued downstairs.

Stepping into the vestibule, the girls heard the soft patter of Miss Peartree's steps descending from the second floor.

"Oh, girls, I'm so glad I caught up with you!" Miss Peartree arrived at the bottom of the stairs and smiled. "I didn't want to ask you about your books in front of Mrs. King at breakfast, but I was wondering if you had a chance to look over the new ones from our meeting yesterday."

Emily shifted on her feet self-consciously, and Evelyn spoke. "Well, you see, Miss Peartree, Emily didn't have much of a chance, since she was finishing up some lacework for Mrs. King. But I read the first chapter of my book; *Rebecca of Sunnybrook Farm* is wonderful!"

"So glad to hear that . . . well, are you two off to church?" Miss Peartree plucked a large hat adorned with ostrich feathers from the coat rack and adjusted it on her head.

"Yes, Miss Peartree. We'll be going across the street to St. Andrew's," Emily answered.

"Very nice. The 'high church' in Stamford. Must remind you of the Church of Ireland. I'm off to the Methodist Church." Miss Peartree pulled open the heavy front door, and the perfume of new grass swept inside. "Ahh, spring is finally here!" Miss Peartree stepped lightly through the door and onto the front porch. Emily and Evelyn followed, breathing in the fresh air. Late morning sun stenciled geometric shadows through the porch rails onto the wooden floor. Bathed in sunshine, the girls stepped down the steps to the sidewalk.

Crossing the street, they opened a wrought iron gate to the fenced cemetery, entering the church property from the back. Evelyn walked swiftly through the graveyard, thinking of Mr. Gargin's fairies and banshees that inhabited places like this.

As they came around to the front of the church building, a stream of church-goers lined up at the arched front doors. Evelyn took in the building, never ceasing to be impressed by the elegant architecture, though she viewed it from her third floor bedroom window every day. A Gothic style building built of stone, it angled in and out with a variety of pitched roof lines, steeples, and turrets.

Once inside, Evelyn and Emily took seats in the middle pew and faced the ornate chancel, enclosed by black and gold iron lattice.

Atop the altar was a golden crucifix that reminded her of Mrs. Kowalski's relics. The wall behind the altar was painted bright blue, glowing from sunlight streaming through kaleidoscopic stained glass windows, a refreshing change from the dreary palate of colors in Mrs. King's house.

Doris and her family arrived and took seats two rows ahead. Doris squirmed, turning around to smile coyly at Evelyn every few minutes. She was dressed in a cream-colored linen dress, and an over-sized bow protruded from her small head like butterfly wings.

The service transported Evelyn back to her family's church in Corbally. St. Andrew's used the same prayer book and hymns. A bittersweet longing swelled in Evelyn's chest as the organ music filled the church.

When the service ended, the congregation left the chapel in groups, greeting each other and chatting. Doris and her mother, Mrs. Beverly King, caught up with Emily and Evelyn outside on the front path of the church.

"Girls, your aunt has invited us to dine with you this afternoon," the younger Mrs. King said, pulling open her parasol to shade her pale skin from the sun.

"Oh, that would be delightful!" Emily said, watching Doris scurry from behind her mother's long skirt to stare at Evelyn.

"Yes, well, Doris is just beside herself with excitement. We shall arrive at three o'clock." Mrs. King looked over her shoulder to locate her husband, who was shaking hands with the rector at the front door.

"We're looking forward to it," Emily said. Evelyn flashed a big smile at Doris.

"I want to go to Evelyn's house now, Mama!" Doris stomped her foot, folded her arms and pouted.

"Now, now, Doris, the girls have lots of cooking to do, I am sure." Reaching into her large purse, she pulled out a rubber baby doll. "Here you go, Dolly needs a bath. Time to go home."

Doris looked at Dolly doubtfully and said, "No, Mama, Dolly is clean. I gave her a bath yesterday." She planted her feet more firmly in the church path.

A look of annoyance began to spread across Mrs. King's face.

Evelyn thought of something. "Doris, if you go home now and change Dolly into her princess clothes, you can come back to our house to eat supper. And after that, we can have our very own special princess tea party for just Dolly, you, and me." Evelyn bent down to Doris's eye level and addressed Dolly directly. "Don't you want to go to a tea party, Dolly?"

"Oh, could we? Mom, let's hurry home! Dolly needs to get her gown!" Doris took her mother's hand and pulled her down the pathway. Ralph King had to run at top speed, holding down his bowler hat, to catch up with them.

Emily laughed, "You sure have a way with that child, Evelyn. Reminds me of the time you got that dog on the ship to stop his howling." Evelyn nodded, remembering Linwood.

The girls hurried home to find Mrs. King waiting at the front door.

"Did Beverly tell you the plan for supper today, girls?" Mrs. King asked, a wooden spoon in her hand, and an apron tied around her waist.

"Yes, Mrs. King. We'll be having guests: Beverly, Ralph, and Doris," Emily answered.

"And that means we had better start supper preparations. While you two were at church, I stuffed a turkey and put it in the oven. Potatoes need to be boiled, cucumber and onion salad diced, and I'd like you to make some apple crisp for dessert, Emily. Do you remember how to make it?"

"Yes, Mrs. King. We'll get started right away." Emily hung her shawl on the coat rack, and Evelyn followed her into the kitchen.

"Evelyn, you can peel the potatoes, while I slice the apples. There's a barrel of apples in the cellar, next to the potatoes and onions, I believe," Emily said, leading the way down the dark cellar stairs to fetch supplies. Evelyn stayed close by, shivering at the thought that something might be lurking in the dark corners. Returning to the kitchen, they began their tasks.

This would be a large meal, with the extra guests and all of the boarders. Mrs. King planned to have the girls serve the boarders first, clearing away their food and dishes before serving her family on the best china. Evelyn noticed that Mrs. King reserved her good mood for her sons, and was quite lavish in the preparation of this meal.

Once the boarders and invalids had been fed, the guests arrived. Doris ran in the door ahead of her parents, clutching Dolly, whose gown dragged upon the floor.

"Evelyn, Evelyn, we're here!" Doris shouted, looking in every direction for her favorite companion.

"Doris, you need to sit at the supper table before you play. Come with me to the dining room." Ralph and Beverly King led their daughter to the table where Evelyn waited with a platter of turkey.

Doris hopped up and down when she spied Evelyn, and her mother settled her into a chair. The little girl's head swiveled in Evelyn's directions, tracking her every move.

Mrs. King asked Ralph to lead them in grace and after, the family ate. Emily and Evelyn served food and kept busy refilling beverage glasses.

Ralph had just started a career as a lawyer and dominated the conversation with stories from his job. He spoke in a bombastic tone, although he hardly lived the life of a rich lawyer at the moment. He did not yet own a motor car, but many of his associates did, and Ralph relayed some jokes he'd heard at work.

"Did you hear the joke about the Ford and the speedometer?" Ralph asked, tipping back in the armed chair at the head of the table. Since no one had, he continued. "Well, you see, this fellow asks another fellow who happens to own a Flivver, 'Can I sell you a speedometer?'

"Fellow says, 'I don't need one. When my Ford is running five miles an hour, the fender rattles; twelve miles an hour, my teeth rattle; and fifteen miles an hour, the transmission drops out.'"

Everyone at the table laughed, and Doris turned to smile at Evelyn. She waved her fork at Evelyn and Evelyn waved a finger back.

Lester said, "Fellow at the market by the name of Turnball told me a good one. Have you heard about why Ford is the best family car?"

"No, haven't heard that one," Ralph answered.

"It has a tank for father, a hood for mother, and a rattle for baby." Lester guffawed a little too loudly, his mouth still full of food.

"Yes, well, one day soon, when I get my practice off the ground, Doris and her Mama will be driving around in something better than a Flivver." Ralph raised a glass of beer and emptied it to the bottom. He held it up for Emily to refill, a belch erupting from his mouth.

Supper and dessert done, the girls barely had a bite to eat in between, but Mrs. King kept them hopping.

"Evelyn, Doris is beside herself waiting for you! Come and take my dear grandchild and give us all a moment's peace." Mrs. King tittered, using her sweetest expression in front of her sons.

Emily whispered to Evelyn, "Don't worry about washing the dishes. I'll be fine. Doris is desperate for your attention."

Evelyn nodded and took Doris by the hand. "Look at Dolly's lovely princess gown!" she exclaimed. Doris beamed and followed Evelyn to the parlor.

Earlier in the afternoon, Evelyn had arranged some chipped tea cups and filled an old teapot with sugar water. As the tablecloth she'd used some of her homemade lace that had been deemed unsaleable by Mrs. King. Doris's eyes nearly popped out of her head when she saw the setting for three, with child-sized chairs.

"A tea party for the princesses!" Doris seated herself and set Dolly into the chair beside her.

"Yes, well, Madame, would you care for some tea?" Evelyn asked with her best imitation of a British accent.

Doris was fascinated. "Yes, please." She held up her tea cup and batted her eyelashes as Evelyn poured out the sugar water.

"A spot of tea for the princess. And for you as well?" Evelyn addressed Dolly.

"Dolly wants some, too!" Doris nearly bounced out of her chair in excitement. "Evelyn, you're a princess, too. Sit down here and have your tea." Doris pointed to the small chair beside her.

Evelyn slipped into the chair, raised her teacup with an outstretched pinkie, said, "Delicious!" She watched as Doris imitated her motions, her dimpled hands holding the teacup, concentrating hard to raise her own pinkie.

When Doris tired of the tea party, Evelyn showed her how to fold paper to make fans, flowers, cups: ideas she had gotten from Miss Peartree's book, *The American Girl's Handy Book*. Doris was absolutely fascinated by Evelyn's charms. Evelyn's insides glowed. It felt so good to be adored, and at long last, to play like a little girl.

Chapter 26
News from Home

Springtime finally arrived in Stamford, bringing new hope for Evelyn and Emily. And finally, on one sunny April day, word from home came through the mail slot at 89 Franklin Street.

An ordinary Wednesday afternoon of chores, Evelyn swept out each bedroom stove of ashes. She had looked in on both Mrs. Krieger and Mrs. Kowalski, and fed them a little applesauce and toast. Laundry washed, Evelyn had left it to dry on the clothes line in the backyard. Mrs. King and Emily had left for the market, and Evelyn was to meet them there later, at three o'clock, to help stock some shelves.

But the sound of the mailman lifting the creaky metal door of the mail slot made Evelyn stop in her tracks. Several white envelopes dropped through the slot, and Evelyn raced to the bathroom to wash the soot from her hands. She was desperate for a word from home. It had been two months, the longest stretch so far, without a letter from Ma. Every day when mail arrived, Evelyn had the same rush of expectation, only to be crestfallen at the pile of bills and business letters for Mrs. King.

This time, Evelyn spotted the thin paper envelope her mother used for post. The address was written in her mother's familiar penmanship, and Evelyn noted she'd remembered to use her new name, Evelyn, instead of Winnie.

Evelyn held the envelope to her cheek and breathed in, hoping for a scent of Corbally. She carefully ripped it open, her heart beating so quickly she thought it would pop right out of her chest. Pulling out the paper, she let it unfold and began to read.

My dearest Emily and Evelyn,

The good news is that we are blessed with another daughter. Wee Isabella Weir joined us on March 3. She looks a lot like Winnie did as an infant.

I am sorry to tell you that we have had a very bad winter here in Corbally. Nearly all the cattle are gone, due to disease. The crops are bad, rotten from so much rain. How lucky you are to be in America.

Annie's leg is as good as new. She's running after Tommy all day and I'll be using her help with wee Bella.

Da sends his love. You know he is not much of a writer. He leaves that to me. Heaven knows he misses you both. Da works so hard. He wants you to know that we plan to join you girls, but will be delayed for at least one year or more, what with the baby and difficulties at the farm.

We hope and pray that you are well. Put your trust in the Lord.

May God bless you,
Ma

Tears streaked down Evelyn's sooty cheeks, making clean tracks to her jaw line. A new baby sister. Annie is better. Failing crops and dead cattle. At least one more year. Maybe two. Evelyn's chest heaved and a floodgate of tears burst.

Without Emily to console her, she reread the letter over and over, just to be sure she'd gotten it right.

Knowing that Mrs. King would be angry if she did not complete her chores and arrive at the market on time, Evelyn forced herself to walk up the stairs to the bathroom and splash cold water on her face.

Seeing her dirty anguished face in the mirror, Evelyn shuddered. She must keep herself together. One more year. Maybe two.

As she dried her face with a towel, she heard a low murmur from Mrs. Kowalski's room. Hesitating, she turned towards the old lady's door and listened. Yes, Mrs. Kowalski was making noises. Evelyn knocked on the door, "Mrs. Kowalski, are you all right?"

No answer. Evelyn walked in and saw Mrs. Kowalski propped up in bed. Her blue eyes grew round and locked on Evelyn. "Clara?"

"It's me, Evelyn. Are you all right?" Evelyn asked, stepping closer.

"Clara . . ." Mrs. Kowalski made a noise that sounded a bit like crying. Evelyn noticed wetness in the creases of the old lady's temples.

"Is there anything I can do?" Evelyn took one last look at the room, and noticed that the trunk was sticking out further from its usual position. She pushed it back into place with the toe of her pointy black work shoe.

Mrs. Kowalski pulled a blanket up to her neck and rolled onto her side, closing her eyes.

Evelyn said, "I'll be back at supper time, Mrs. Kowalski."

Leaving the room, Evelyn wondered how on earth that trunk had moved again.

Entering the kitchen, Evelyn noticed the time: two o'clock. She'd have just enough time to pull down the clean laundry from the line, fold it, and walk to the market by three.

Once the laundry was done, she stepped through the front door and let the spring sunshine warm her face. Buds punctuated the ends of the branches of a hydrangea bush in the front yard. Crocuses popped up cheerfully throughout the lawn. A yellow forsythia bush divided Mrs. King's property from a tavern next door. Evelyn saw Mr. Walker stumbling through the tavern doorway, wincing in the bright sunlight.

She hurried in the opposite direction towards Pacific Street. Passing by Doris's row house, she noticed Dolly propped against a bedroom window. In the front yard child-sized table and chairs had been arranged for outdoor picnics. Evelyn patted her sweater pocket to make sure that Ma's letter was still there. She'd slip it to Emily in the back room at the market. Emily would feel just as badly about the news, but she'd say just the right thing to make Evelyn feel better.

Rounding the corner of Pacific Street, Evelyn spied Mr. Santoriello inside the barber shop, shaving a customer. Waving as she scurried by, he saw her, and raised a hand holding a razor, calling, "Good day, Evelyn!"

In front of the market, several horse and carts were parked, delivery boys unloading goods. A motor car pulled away, an advertisement on its side read, "Klein and Gmahle: Finest Meat Products."

Entering the store, Evelyn saw Lester at the register, slumped on his chair, looking bored.

Some customers walked the aisles, collecting cans and packages in their shopping baskets. Mrs. King looked up from her desk in the back room as Evelyn approached. "Evelyn, come along. There are packages to sort out here."

Evelyn met eyes with Emily, who was perched atop a tall stool, a tablet in one hand, pen in the other.

Mrs. King said, "Move that box to the left. You need to straighten out this shelf for a proper display." Evelyn busied herself with moving boxes. A customer interrupted Mrs. King with a question, leaving Evelyn alone with Emily for a moment.

Evelyn whispered, "A letter from Ma came today."

She reached inside her pocket and handed it to Emily as discreetly as possible.

"Is it good news?" Emily asked, taking the paper to her lap.

Evelyn barely had a chance to shake her head "no" when Mrs. King returned and said, "Now then, Evelyn, no more dilly-dallying. Off you go!"

Stacking cans of vegetables on shelves, Evelyn glanced over her shoulder to see if Emily had read the letter. She could just make out the paper on top of Emily's bookkeeping pad. When Mrs. King left the back room to help another customer, Emily looked up at Evelyn. With a sad smile, Emily shook her head, and dabbed a handkerchief at her cheeks.

Although her own eyes welled with tears, Evelyn felt comforted that Emily shared in the disappointment. No words were necessary. Emily's presence was Evelyn's solace.

Chapter 27
August 1914

Evelyn and Emily spent the next four years in a haze of grueling drudgery at 89 Franklin Street, hoping, hoping for good news. And now, in the summer of 1914, the news only got worse.

"ENGLAND DECLARES WAR ON GERMANY!" The headlines screamed from every newsstand along Pacific Street. What else could go wrong? Evelyn reached for a copy of *The New York Times* and *The Stamford Advocate*. As she scanned the front pages, Doris waited patiently by Evelyn's side.

"What's the matter, Evelyn?" Doris asked, her hair ribbon drooping in the August heat.

"Oh, there's bad news from Europe. But don't you worry, you'll be safe here in America." Evelyn smiled weakly, squeezing Doris's hand. Now that school was out for the summer, it was Evelyn's job to care for seven-year-old Doris until her mother came home from work each day. Apparently Ralph was not the successful lawyer he pretended to be, his gambling habits having devoured his income. Beverly was obliged to find work to supplement the family income. Evelyn was delighted to do her part in watching Doris.

"How about a lollipop?" Evelyn asked.

"Oh, could I? Red is my favorite!" Doris hopped up and down

as Evelyn pulled the candy from a box and paid the newsboy with some change.

As Doris licked her lollipop with great gusto, Evelyn sunk into less happy thoughts. She made a mental list of all the reasons her family in Ireland still had not come to Stamford. Another baby brother born last year. No money. Increased danger of ships crossing the Atlantic, now that war had been declared. The idea that she might never see her family again was a dark thought Evelyn had never allowed herself to think. Yet for a fleeting moment, the idea surged to the forefront of her mind like a winged phantom.

Evelyn wiped perspiration from her brow. Was it the heat of this August afternoon, or worry for the future that made her break out in sweat?

Striding down Franklin Street with a grocery bag in one hand, Doris in the other, she willed herself to shove bad thoughts out of the way. "Look, Doris, the hydrangeas have blossomed!" Entering the front yard, she bent over to sniff a snowball sized flower, Doris copying her. "And can't you just smell the cut grass? Mr. Walker must have mowed it today." The green scent put Evelyn back to Da's pastures in Corbally. "What would you say about a quick roll down the slope in the backyard?" Evelyn's eyes twinkled mischievously.

"But Evelyn, you're fourteen years old. You're too old to roll in the grass."

Evelyn didn't bother to correct Doris's mistake about her age. Although she was well past her fifteenth birthday, she remained girlish looking, and was in no rush to become a woman. Emily had once confided in Evelyn that she was also presenting her age as a few years younger. "We've been robbed of four of our best years thanks to Mrs. King and the labor she's made us do. The way I see it, the last few years just don't count." Lord knows Mrs. King wasn't keeping track of such frivolous occasions as birthdays.

Evelyn grinned at Doris, "Everyone knows that you're never too old for grass-rolling!" She grabbed Doris's arm and pulled her to the walkway around to the back of the house, set the grocery bag down on the steps, and ran up a small slope. "Bet you can't catch me!" Doris darted after Evelyn, who was already winding up her arms against her summer smock and rolling downward.

At the bottom of the hill, Evelyn giggled. "See? Wasn't that hill just asking to be rolled down?"

"I didn't hear it say anything." Doris's face grew serious.

"Well, if you stick your ear real close to the ground you might even hear the fairies sing." Evelyn demonstrated with her head pressed sideways against the earth. "Yes, they are singing. About how good it is to have a friend."

"Are they really, Evelyn?" Doris asked, mouth agape.

"Absolutely! Now, I'll bring out a basin of water so that you can give Dolly a bath out here while I start supper."

A horse from the stable let out a loud whiny and Doris ran towards it. "Come, Evelyn, let's say hello to the horse!"

Evelyn caught up with Doris, parting the hanging laundry to pass through to the far corner of the yard. Through the barn window, they patted an old brown mare. Flies circled everywhere, and Evelyn noticed whiskey bottles strewn in the corner of the stable.

"Come, Doris, that's enough. Mr. Walker might be coming back soon, and I don't want to disturb him." The truth was that Evelyn was frightened of Mr. Walker and his drinking. More than a few times since she'd come to Stamford, Mrs. King had ordered Emily and Evelyn to clean up broken glass and other trash from the backyard.

Safely at the backdoor, Evelyn set out a tub of water for Doris to use to bathe Dolly.

"I'll be watching from the window above the sink. But be sure Dolly gets very clean." Evelyn gathered the grocery bags and went inside.

Doris played at the bottom of the backdoor steps as Evelyn emptied the shopping bags of their contents onto the countertop. She had purchased a large sack of sugar so she could stew some of the rhubarb stems she'd picked from the garden earlier today. The green-maroon rhubarb stems softened in the boiling water as she sprinkled a liberal amount of white sugar inside the pot. Raising a spoon to her mouth, she blew until it was cool enough to taste. Slipping the soft warm mixture into her mouth, she savored a moment of sugar-tart pleasure. Busying herself with the rest of the supper preparations, she thought how it had been over four years of this routine, and now she felt quite competent in Mrs. King's kitchen. She set aside a platter of stewed rhubarb for Mrs. Krieger and Mrs. Kowalski. It was a miracle that they had hung on to life for this long. Miss Peartree had said it was to Emily and Evelyn's credit that the ladies had lived all these years. There continued to be some odd episodes of unusual noises and a displaced trunk in Mrs. Kowalski's room. Yet, whenever Evelyn looked in on her, the old lady was as vacant as ever. Maybe she was just imagining it . . . Emily often told her that she had a very active imagination.

Doris called from the back step, "I'm hungry, Evelyn!"

"How about some rhubarb for you and Dolly?"

Doris scooped up a dripping Dolly and ran straightway to the kitchen.

"You didn't waste a minute, did you?" Evelyn laughed, handing Doris a small bowl. Doris dug in hungrily.

Someone knocked at the front door, and Doris said, "It's Mama. I can see her hat shape through the glass." Sure enough, Beverly King was standing at the door, looking flushed and hot from her walk home from work.

"Hello, Evelyn, and where is that daughter of mine?" Beverly said, propping her parasol on the coat rack.

Doris ran and hugged her mother, looking over her shoulder at Evelyn.

"Will I play with Evelyn again tomorrow, Mama?"

"Yes, dear, of course. Thank you, Evelyn. We shall see you again tomorrow morning." Doris followed her mother, Dolly tucked in her armpit, drops of water trailing down the hallway. She took one last look at Evelyn and said, "Evelyn, tomorrow can we play dress-up and hopscotch and buy ice cream from the ice cream man and build fairy houses?"

"Of course!" laughed Evelyn.

Now that she was alone in the kitchen, Evelyn once again considered the news of war. She had an overwhelming sense of worry for her family. Silently repeating some of Miss Peartree's aphorisms, she tried to make sense of the future. *Hope springs eternal. Patience is a virtue. Blessed are all they that put their trust in Him.*

Emily arrived home from the market and joined Evelyn in the kitchen.

"I suppose you've heard the news of war, Evelyn." Emily's face was laden with fear.

"Yes. I've got the newspaper to read later."

"It's all everyone is talking about at the market." Emily hugged herself, then resumed her kitchen chores.

One by one, the boarders entered the house, home from their jobs, the buzz of war news in the air.

"Very bad news, very bad," Evelyn heard Mr. Santoriello say as he entered the hall.

"The Brits will get rid of those Krauts. No problem," came Lester's voice.

"We must pray that the war is over soon," answered Mr. Santoriello.

Evelyn knew he was desperately worried for his family left behind in Italy. It was a feeling she knew only too well.

Supper served, dishes cleaned, invalids settled for the night, Evelyn wiped a damp cloth across her hot forehead. Making her way up to the third floor bedroom late that night, gaslight in hand to light the way, she was hit by a wall of stagnant hot air.

Setting the gaslight on the bureau under the tiny front window, Evelyn raised the sash and thought about opening her latest book from Miss Peartree: *Little Women.* She loved this book, with its homey tales of a big family. Sisters, mother, father . . . But she really needed to keep up with the news of the war. Miss Peartree had taught the girls the importance of staying informed of current events. Evelyn could never forget the Saturday meeting three years ago where Miss Peartree had shared a newspaper article about the Titanic disaster. The tragedy became even more real as Evelyn considered that her ship had traveled the same course. Despite the night's heat, she shivered to think of a huge ship plunging into the icy waters of the Atlantic. She remembered the chill of the night air, the murky black waters.

Shaking out the paper in front of her, Evelyn began to read about the new menace of war.

Emily entered the room, having just taken a bath, but looking as hot as ever.

"My goodness, hot air sure rises in this old house! I didn't think it could be any hotter than the kitchen, but apparently I was wrong. The air in this room is like the devil's breath itself!" She raised the window as high as it would go, and a slight breeze drifted in, pulling the muslin curtains in and out, as though they were breathing. "There now, I think that might help. Feels like a refreshing one hundred degrees now, down from one hundred and twenty."

Emily sat on her side of the bed, bending at her waist to rub her feet. Her bunions had been bothering her lately.

Evelyn read some of the news articles aloud to Emily. "British ship sunk; French ships defeat German, Belgium attacked; 17,000,000 men engaged in great war of eight nations; Great English and German navies about to grapple; rival warships off this port as Lusitania sails ..."

Suddenly, the smell of something burning interrupted Evelyn's reading.

Looking up, she saw that the edge of a curtain had blown into the gas lamp and caught fire.

"Oh, no, Emily, look the curtain is on fire!" Evelyn's face blanched in fear.

Emily jumped up and answered, "Hush, now don't go waking the whole house. I can get it out without Mrs. King ever finding out." She ran to the curtain and began to swat the flames with nothing but her bare hands.

"Em, you're going to hurt yourself!" Evelyn watched in horror as orange flames licked at her sister's hands.

"Never you mind, the flames are out, and no one has been troubled by it," Emily said, her voice catching on a stab of pain and nausea, as the putrid smell of burned flesh collected in the bedroom. She swallowed hard, a look of horror on her face as she surveyed her blackened palms. "Oh, no," she moaned, blowing on her hands, and waving them around.

Evelyn jumped out of bed and grabbed a cloth. "I'll fetch some cool water from the tap so you can soak your hands." Gathering a basin and rags, she looked back at Emily and asked, "Are you all right?"

Emily nodded and said in a weak voice, "I'm all right. Water would be nice." Tears ran down her cheeks. Evelyn had never seen Emily in so much pain.

Running down the stairs to the second floor lavatory, Evelyn realized how she had always taken Emily's strength for granted. Emily was now a pretty young woman, being courted by several young men the market. Seeing her capable and confident sister break down was more jarring than a war across the ocean.

Returning with a pitcher of water and some salve from the medicine cabinet, Evelyn remembered how Emily had comforted her through all the hard times.

"Here you go, Em, sit down on the edge of the bed." Evelyn guided Emily and sat beside her. "Dip your hands in this water."

Emily's tense muscles released as the cool water soothed the pain.

"Just keep your hands in there and I'll get some salve for you to wrap on your wounds." After a time, Evelyn carefully took Emily's hands into her lap and gently wrapped damp soft rags around her hands.

"It's getting late, Em. Why don't you let me undo your buttons, so you can put on your night gown and get some sleep."

Emily nodded and allowed Evelyn to undress her and tuck her into bed.

"I'll leave this basin of water beside you all night. You might need to soak your hands to relieve the pain." Evelyn patted a light sheet over Emily as she settled into bed.

Emily turned to her. "You know, Evelyn, it was not very long ago that you were a squirming little girl named Winnie, sitting on a stool as I battled the tangles out of your hair. Seems to me little Winnie was left behind in Corbally, and now I've got a young lady named Evelyn as my sister. And it's a good thing. I need the help of a capable woman!"

Evelyn leaned her head against Emily's shoulder, careful not to disturb her burned hands. "Em?"

"What, Evelyn?"

"Tomorrow, let me do all your chores."

"You won't have to twist my arm," Emily laughed, but then winced, her hands throbbing. "Goodnight, Evelyn."

Evelyn leaned over to blow out the gaslight. She took one last look at her sister. Sadness and joy mixed in her heart like silt and spring water in the bottom of a very deep well. "I love you, Em."

Chapter 28
July 1919

As Evelyn gazed at her reflection in the mirror above the lavatory sink, she decided that finally she looked like a grown woman. She was twenty-one years of age, but if asked, she'd probably say she was eighteen. She brushed her hand self-consciously across her protruding front teeth. Sighing, she hoped the old adage was true: *Beautiful is as beautiful does.* From the recesses of her memory she conjured an image of Da's toothy smile. Taking a brush to her newly coifed short hair, she wondered if Emily was right that her entrance to womanhood had been delayed.

"It's all the toil and back-breaking labor Mrs. King has made you do all these years." Emily had often worried at how child-like Evelyn's body had remained, despite the passing years. Evelyn was not as worried. She needed time to make up for lost moments of girlhood. She and Doris, seven years her junior, had grown especially close, and were often mistaken for being the same age.

But earlier this week at the market, a peculiar thing had happened that made her wish to look more beautiful. As she had squatted beside a box of cans to be shelved, she had felt a single hair on her scalp prickle, as if someone had carefully plucked just one. A whisper of air behind her. When she turned to look, no one was there, just a delivery boy leaving through the door. When she resumed her task, she thought she felt the boy turn to glance at her, but when she looked back up, all she could see was a flash of jet black hair escaping from his cap. A strange new feeling came over her. Her face got hot and her insides flipped. She didn't know why, but she really wanted to see that boy's face.

Evelyn started down the stairs to begin a day of cleaning, when Miss Peartree emerged from her room. "Evelyn, you're looking well today!" Miss Peartree pushed her glasses against her face, a pen in one hand. "I have a question for you. Have you had a chance to register to vote?"

Evelyn gulped. She knew how excited Miss Peartree was when last month Congress had passed an amendment to allow women the right to vote. But even now, Evelyn couldn't get past her fear of Mrs. King's warnings about the authorities. Throughout the years, Miss Peartree had badgered her to get her citizenship. Evelyn had pretended to do it last year, but fear of Mrs. King kept her from actually getting it. She found herself dodging the issue once again, "Yes, Miss Peartree, I'll be sure to register this week."

"Well, I certainly hope so. It is every woman's right and responsibility to vote."

Evelyn never thought she'd be glad to see Mrs. King, but today she was relieved to see her stepping from her bedroom. Mrs. King was dressed in black, a dark veil covering her face.

"Good morning, Mrs. King," Evelyn said.

"Good morning, Mrs. King," Miss Peartree said, curiously regarding Mrs. King's black veil.

Just then, Emily descended the stairs to join them.

"Yes, well, it's not the best morning. I received sad news last night. Mr. King has passed on." Evelyn and Emily swapped a quick look of shock.

"So sorry to hear the sad news, Mrs. King," Emily said.

"Yes, we are very sorry," added Evelyn, slightly flustered.

Miss Peartree said, "You have my condolences, Mrs. King."

Mrs. King looked the girls straight in the eyes and said, "Well, since he was your uncle, I will expect you to put on your mourning clothes to attend the funeral and pay your respects, of course."

Evelyn absorbed this news with confused feelings. Mr. King had remained a remote background figure in her life. She had never actually met him, although she thought she had spotted him a few times at the market, exchanging some words with Lester at the cash register. But no one had ever introduced her to him. In fact, everyone seemed to go out of their way not to mention him, especially not in front of Mrs. King.

"We'll be right down in our dresses, Mrs. King," Emily said, grabbing Evelyn's arm as she turned up the stairs.

"I'd like to attend, as well, if that would be all right with you," Miss Peartree said.

"Yes, very well, then. Service is at ten o'clock at St. Andrew's." Evelyn thought she heard a slight break in Mrs. King's steel voice.

Once upstairs with the door closed, Evelyn asked, "Emily, what do you think about Mr. King?" After all these years of avoiding this taboo subject, it felt peculiar to mention Mr. King's name.

"Well, as much as I can surmise, Mrs. King and he couldn't get along, so they took matters into their own hands. Lived their lives apart and moved on."

"Seems so, but I wonder if Mrs. King really ever 'moved on'. I mean she always seems so angry about something. Maybe she's been angry at Mr. King all these years." Evelyn blinked at her own audacity.

"You may be right, but it doesn't change anything now, does it? We'll let Mrs. King have her day to mourn. But it's not the death of Mr. King she is probably mourning, it's more likely the death of some dream she had a long time ago."

"Now you are talking like Miss Peartree, Em. What do you mean?"

"I mean, Mrs. King was young once. I'm sure she had dreams. Da remembers her as a lovely young woman. She must have suffered a huge disappointment to become so cold and angry."

"I'll never understand her." Evelyn pulled down her black dress and smoothed the fabric. She cinched the waste with a belt, looking in the mirror. Taking a brush to her bobbed hair, she heard the sound of the mailman slipping letters into the slot.

"No, Evelyn, not only will you never understand her, you'll never be like her either. Your heart is far too big." Emily primped her short stylish hair, and added, "Look at the time ... it's nearly ten o'clock. We'd better run."

The funeral service was sparsely attended. Mrs. King's family filled two pews, the boarders sat behind, and a sprinkling of older men, presumably business associates, dotted the rest of the chapel.

After a somber meal with Ralph, Beverly, Doris, and Lester, the girls started upstairs to tend the old ladies. As they rounded the banister, Evelyn spotted a pile of unopened mail.

"Em, let me check the mail first." Evelyn did not expect much from the mail any more. Letters from home were faithful, but few and far between. Annie had taken a position as a servant more than sixty miles away in the house of a wealthy family near Belfast. Thirteen-year-old Tommy and Da ran the farm, and Bella helped Ma out at home with five-year-old Robert. During these last five years, there had been no chance of a trip across the Atlantic with German U-boats sinking anything that moved in the water. Why, even the California had fallen prey to the Germans, sinking off the coast of Ireland two years ago.

"Oh, good, a letter from Ma," she exclaimed, as she flipped through the stack of envelopes.

Ripping open the envelope, Evelyn readied herself to read the usual news of farm life in Corbally. And maybe, just maybe, now that the Great War was over, there'd be news of a reunion.

> *Dearest Emily and Evelyn,*
>
> *It is with deepest regret that I write to you today. Your dear father has been taken from us and is with the Lord now. The terrible influenza epidemic has swept through Ulster and your poor Da, with his weak heart, could not fight it. Thank God the rest of us were spared.*
>
> *We are beside ourselves at the loss of your Da. He was a good husband and a man of integrity. Thankfully, your grandda and grandma Moffat have been very helpful to me and the children.*
>
> *Pray for us and know that we pray for you.*
> *Yours in sympathy,*
> *Ma*

Evelyn blinked fiercely, trying to rid her eyes of fog. This could not have happened. Da said he would come. And she had waited more than ten years. She no longer felt like a grown-up. She felt like an abandoned eleven-year-old girl.

Her face burned as she ran up the stairs, fighting back tears, she passed Emily. "What is it, Evelyn?" Emily froze in place when she saw the look on her sister's face.

Evelyn threw the paper to Emily and continued up the stairs to her room, slamming the door shut, hurling her body onto the bed.

She retched into a basin, coughing and sputtering from the shock.

Emily slipped inside the door, her face pale and tear-stained. "Evelyn?"

"There's nothing anyone can say, Em . . . I just don't know how I'll go on." Evelyn groped for Emily's embrace and the sisters wept in each other's arms.

Chapter 29
Mrs. Kowalski

The rasp of Mrs. Kowalski's voice interrupted Evelyn and Emily's grief.

Emily turned to listen. "Evelyn, do you hear that?"

Holding a hanky to her nose, Evelyn nodded yes.

"I think I'd better go look in on Mrs. Krieger and Mrs. Kowalski. It's past their usual check time." Emily dabbed at her eyes with the edge of her apron.

"Em, I'll go down and check on Mrs. Kowalski. It's my job. She'll be upset if there's any change to her routine." Evelyn burrowed her blotchy face into the hanky and blew her nose.

"Are you sure you want to go down now? You've hardly had a chance to absorb our sad news."

"I'll never get over this, Em," Evelyn said, tucking the hanky away. "There's nothing left for me to hope for. Ma will never take the trip without Da. It was his dream."

"I'm afraid you're right." Emily gazed at Evelyn with pain in her eyes.

"Now all we're left with is this drudge." Evelyn eyes welled up with more tears.

Again, the gravelly sound of Mrs. Kowalski's voice calling.

Evelyn turned to the door. "I'll go down to her, but I'd like you to come after you've looked in on Mrs. Krieger. In case there's anything wrong."

When Evelyn arrived at the door, she could hear Mrs. Kowalski moaning even louder. This time she rushed in without knocking.

"What is it, Mrs. Kowalski?"

The old lady looked up her with wild eyes and muttered some Polish words, ending with, "Clara!"

"Yes, yes, I know you miss her. You must be very sad. But you are here in Stamford in Mrs. King's boarding house." Just then, Emily stepped in next to Evelyn. "I am Evelyn, and this is Emily." Evelyn used her hands to indicate each person.

Mrs. Kowalski's manic eyes raced across the girls' bodies and suddenly fixed upon Evelyn's face. "Evelyn . . ." she whispered and reached out her hand.

Evelyn moved in closer, looking back at Emily, not sure if she had heard correctly. Evelyn put her hand inside Mrs. Kowalski's gnarled grasp. The old lady pulled her to the bed, this time her blue eyes were lucid, locking onto Evelyn's tear-stained eyes.

"Evelyn ... good girl." She shut her eyes and stopped breathing.

"Mrs. Kowalski?" Evelyn panicked and put her hand to the woman's chest. No pulse.

"Oh, Emily, this is too much!" She sped out the room and up the stairs to finish the grieving she'd barely started.

Evelyn fell asleep crying, and woke hours later with a raging headache. The letter from Ma lay on the bed beside her. Emily was nowhere to be seen, but she could hear voices in Mrs. Kowalski's room below. She straightened out her apron, and splashed water on her eyes. She ran a comb quickly through her short hair, and saw her puffy face in the mirror. She felt guilty at her self-indulgent crying, knowing that Emily had as much to be sad about as she.

She hurried down the stairs, and timidly faced the open door to Mrs. Kowalski's room. She could see Mrs. King talking to Emily. Spotting Evelyn, Mrs. King waved her to come in.

"Yes, now Evelyn, we are all having quite a time today. First, it's Mr. King, next it's my poor brother in Ireland, and now Mrs. Kowalski." She tsked. Evelyn thought it was an attempt at sounding sympathetic. "Now, Mrs. Kowalski's body has been removed by an ambulance. We've taken care of that, and then there will be the arrangements for a burial. Poor woman had no relations left, so far as I know. I've been instructing Emily to go through the room and pack up her belongings. Strip the bed, open the trunk, the bureau, and fill these boxes with her things. Throw away most of it, but we'll save anything worthwhile, to pay for the burial expenses. Set aside jewelry, watches, things of that nature."

"Yes, Mrs. King," Emily replied, eyes darting towards Evelyn.

"Busy day, busy day," Mrs. King left the room, muttering to herself.

"Emily, it feels wrong to go through her stuff," Evelyn said, sitting on the edge of the mattress.

"I know what you mean. Let's get this over with as fast as possible."

Going through the bureau, the girls filled boxes with clothing they had laundered through the years, they made a separate box of the holy relics and photographs. Labor was nearly as natural as breathing for Evelyn and Emily, a slight distraction from their sorrow.

When it came time to open the trunk, Evelyn paused.

"Em, help me pull this old trunk out from under the bed."

The two young women pulled and the trunk made a somewhat familiar sound of sandpaper on wood.

Unlatching the hook, the trunk popped open to expose folded dresses from another era. "These are beautiful, aren't they?" Evelyn held up a bright red skirt, with striped with ribbons the colors of the rainbow. There were a few necklaces and a pocket watch that Evelyn reluctantly set aside for Mrs. King.

When the trunk was empty, Emily said, "Well, that's done."

Evelyn took one last look at the trunk and noticed a side compartment bulging slightly. "No, Em, I think there's more in here."

Opening it, she found brittle papers filled with Polish writing.

"That can just go in the trash, Evelyn," Emily said, absentmindedly dusting off the empty bureau.

"Wait . . . I wonder . . . Em, I'd like to keep these papers, in case there's a story here. You never know."

"Sure. Why don't you add them to the small box with some of the Polish dresses for Doris to use for dress-up? Mrs. King is only interested in jewels."

Evelyn set aside the ribbon skirt, the photograph, and the papers, thinking of how she could find out what these Polish words said. She had an idea. "Em, if we're done now, I'd like to pay Miss

Peartree a visit."

"That would be fine. I'll be down in the kitchen starting supper."

Holding the box in front of her, Evelyn took a shaky breath. Da had died. She was left in Stamford to have a life. Without the rest of her family. With Emily.

Chapter 30
Hints of Harold

Evelyn paused in front of Miss Peartree's door, box in hand. She set the box down to swipe a hanky across her nose once more. Inhaling deeply, she knocked.

"Coming!" came the sing-song voice of Miss Peartree.

Opening the door, Miss Peartree's face softened in sympathy and she said, "Oh come here, you poor dear. What an awful day for you!" She embraced Evelyn and patting her back, said, "Why don't you come in and have a seat? I miss our weekly book meetings and it's been ages since we've had a moment together to talk."

Miss Peartree guided a wobbly kneed Evelyn to a set of chairs beside a window. Evelyn could see the shingled side of the tavern, and hear the faint sound of drunken men shouting and laughing. Not a sound she wanted to hear.

Miss Peartree noticed Evelyn's distraction from the noise and went to close the curtain.

"There, now, Evelyn, I am so very, very sorry to hear about the loss of your father. This has been quite a day. And poor Mrs. Kowalski. I'd never have thought Mrs. Krieger would outlive her."

"Thank you, Miss Peartree. This has been an awful day for me." Swallowing back tears, Evelyn added, "But there is one thing you might be able to help me with." She reached into the box and pulled out the brittle papers.

"I was wondering if you knew anyone who could translate these letters. They were in Mrs. Kowalski's trunk, and I think they were important to her. I've been so curious all these years about her ranting in Polish, and why she kept calling me Clara. Do you think you could find someone to do this?"

Miss Peartree smiled and said, "I know just the person. The third grade teacher is Mrs. Dombrowski, and she lives with her parents who speak fluent Polish. I'll ask her tomorrow at school to take them home. Maybe we'll solve your mystery."

Evelyn felt a slight smile spread across her face, the first in a long time. "Thank you so much, Miss Peartree."

"No trouble at all. And by the way, Evelyn, I know how heartbroken you must be to hear about your father. But please remember that America holds so much promise for a bright young woman like yourself." Patting Evelyn's shoulder, she added, "Remember, our greatest glory is not in never falling, but in rising every time we fall."

Evelyn left Miss Peartree and met Emily upstairs in their bedroom.

"Emily, are you sure that Ma will never make the trip to America? The war is over."

"Evelyn, I know this is not what you want to hear; but 'no,' she would never make a change like that without Da. In fact, she is probably getting more and more support from Grandma and Grandda Moffat. She mentioned that in her letter. America was Da's dream, but Ma was born a Moffat, proud to be an Ulsterman, a member of the British Kingdom. The Moffats have a different way of thinking."

"I know in my heart that you are right. But for all these years, I've held out hope. Now I feel like there's nothing left."

"Evelyn, you've blossomed into a pretty young woman, despite my worries about the work affecting your growth." With a sly smile, she said, "You know Henry told me something that may be of interest to you." Henry Klein was Emily's new beau; they'd met at King's market. He worked for his family's meat processing company, and often made deliveries to Mrs. King's market. "He says that a fellow named Harold Howard has been pestering him to get your name."

Evelyn shot a confused look at Emily. Could Harold be the delivery boy with the jet black hair? "Well, I don't know anyone by that name . . ."

"No, you don't, but if you'd pay closer attention, you might notice him coming through the store for one of his deliveries. He's certainly noticed you!"

Evelyn blushed and considered this. But a cloak of grief smothered her thoughts of Harold. "I've spent all this time expecting my life to be so different. But now, here I am . . ." Her voice broke off in a spasm of crying.

"No, Evelyn, it's not 'here I am,' it's 'here we are.' You know I've always told you I'll stay by your side."

"Yes, but what is to become of me when you get married? If Henry had his way, you'd be married tomorrow."

"Evelyn, you know as well as I that Mrs. King has her iron grip on my life. Henry and I still have not figured out a way to get around her. But as soon as we do, you're coming along with us." Grinning mischievously, she added, "And we wouldn't mind if you brought along Harold as well!"

"Oh, Emily, I've never even seen this fellow's face! You shouldn't say such things." Evelyn couldn't help herself from smiling. A tiny ember of hope began to warm the hollow in her heart.

Evelyn spent the next week in a daze. She tried desperately to sort out her feelings about never seeing Da again, and for that matter, no one else in her family from Corbally. She felt duped.

She never would have agreed to come to America in the first place had she known there'd be no reunion. On the other hand, Annie's fate in staying behind seemed so dull, just a servant job miles and miles away from home. Not so different from Evelyn in Stamford. But it was different: Annie was in Ireland and Evelyn was in America. And Evelyn had become fond of the many wonders of America. The wealth and variety of food, clothing, houses, possessions. The hope in the eyes of immigrants who would make their fortunes in businesses through hard work. Opportunity. She thought for a moment that she finally understood Da's dream. And then there were her dear friends: Miss Peartree and Doris. And Emily.

Of course, there was that young man . . . Harold. Once again at the market, she'd felt a single hair prickle on her scalp. Quickly turning to look, Evelyn had captured a glimpse of a delivery boy slipping away and out the door to a horse and cart. Was he pulling her hair to show affection? Rushing to the front window, she'd seen a mischievous glint in his blue eyes as he turned to look back at her. She was speechless.

One Friday evening, as the girls readied themselves for bed, Evelyn heard a polite rap at their door, followed by Miss Peartree's voice, "Evelyn? It's me, Miss Peartree."

"Oh, do come in!" Evelyn rushed to open the door. Miss Peartree entered, clutching a folder containing yellowed papers.

"Sorry to disturb you so late, but I've just returned from the Women's Club meeting down at the Ferguson Library. Mrs. Dombrowski was there as well, and I've got some information for you." She opened the folder and smoothed some papers.

"Please tell us, Miss Peartree." Evelyn gestured for her to sit on the edge of the bed, as there was nowhere else to sit in the room. Emily and Evelyn took places on either side.

"Yes, well, to summarize, Mrs. Kowalski's life could surely be called a cautionary tale. Mrs. Dombrowski said that the letters are correspondence between Mrs. Kowalski and her sister, Clara. Seems as if they had been very close when they lived in Poland, and continued correspondence when Mrs. Kowalski married and came to America. Mr. and Mrs. Kowalski ran a successful business years ago, here in Stamford. He was a tailor, and she was a seamstress. Back in Poland, Clara had fallen in love and married a Jewish man, much to the family's disapproval, Mr. and Mrs. Kowalski included. After that, the letters were one way: Clara to Mrs. Kowalski in America. Mrs. Kowalski never responded, although she did save all of her sister's letters. Basically, Clara and her husband fell on hard times and pleaded for help from Mrs. Kowalski and her husband. Help with money so that they could escape the prejudices of the Czarist regime in Eastern Poland and come here. Like so many others, they yearned to live in our free country. Unfortunately, Mr. and Mrs. Kowalski refused to help, holding onto those same old prejudices. Sadly, Clara and her husband were massacred in a pogrom. We know this because there is one last letter written posthumously to Clara by Mrs. Kowalski. In it she expresses unbearable regret that she hadn't set aside her prejudices and allowed Clara and her husband to join her in America. Soon after Clara's sad fate, Mr. Kowalski died. Mrs. Kowalski must have suffered greatly from the losses, the business went under, and she used what money she had left to pay Mrs. King for the boarding house. The rest you know."

Evelyn tilted her head, absorbing the story. "That is a sad story. Poor Mrs. Kowalski must have been so tormented that she mustered the strength to open that heavy trunk. Hiding those papers from us all these years. But why in heaven's name wouldn't she have helped her own sister?"

"Of course you couldn't understand that, Evelyn. You are made of different stuff. Poor Mrs. Kowalski's life was a lesson for us all. She wasted away from regret. Died with a broken heart." Miss Peartree shook her head and gathered together the papers, handing them to Evelyn. "I'd better be off to bed. I hope that satisfies your curiosity, Evelyn. A sad, sad story, but my, doesn't it shed light on how fortunate we are?" Miss Peartree stepped lightly down the steps. Evelyn remained sitting on the edge of the bed, deep in thought.

"Emily, I can't help but remember Da's tale about Ma and when they got married. Remember the part about Grandda Moffat disowning his own daughter for marrying a Scotsman?"

Emily shook her head. "Isn't that awful? Da was right. There is so much more hope in America. And can you imagine what Grandda Moffat would say if he knew about Henry Klein? A German?!" Emily giggled, and added, "At least Henry's a Protestant German. Heaven help Grandda if your Harold turns out to be a Catholic!"

A click on the glass window made them stop their conversation.

"What was that?" Evelyn asked, hopping off the bed and rushing to the window.

"Sounded like a pebble on the glass," Emily answered, following.

Squinting through the dark night and looking down, Evelyn spotted a young man, his chiseled features illuminated by the street light. His face was almost Indian-like, his shiny black hair hung like fringe from under his cap. So handsome! He grinned up at her and waved, then turned to jump on a cart. He raised the whip and his horse pulled the cart away from the curb and down Franklin Street.

"Who was that?" Emily asked as they watched the horse and cart turn down North Street.

"I'm not sure . . ." Evelyn felt heat coming to her face, and Emily's lit up with recognition.

"Why, Evelyn, that was Harold! I recognize his cart. That old horse is so ornery, no one can but Harold can get close to it. Henry told me all about it." She broke into a huge grin. "Evelyn, something tells me that you've just found yourself a good man."

Evelyn was stunned that this handsome young man had gone out of his way just for her. Maybe the future wouldn't be quite so bleak.

Epilogue
Wonders Wrought
West North Avenue, Stamford, CT
1933

Seated at Emily's dining room table, Evelyn poured herself some tea into a rose-patterned china cup. From the kitchen she could hear Emily rustling around the inside of the icebox.

"Would you like some toast?" Emily dipped her face through the doorway.

"Sure, that would be wonderful," answered Emily.

"Is Bobby still asleep?" Emily lowered her voice as she stepped into the dining room to get a better view of her one-and-a-half-year-old nephew.

"Yes, he's a sound sleeper. Such a good boy." Evelyn's face broke into a proud smile.

"That he is. We expect big things of that boy, don't we?" Emily whispered.

"I do have high hope that he'll excel. You remember how Ma inspired us about the importance of education. And how important the church was to Da. It would be my hope that Bobby would favor going into the ministry."

"Well, imagine that, Bobby, your mother has already selected your career for you! You're off to a good start, I can tell you that." Emily looked lovingly at Bobby's damp curls on the side of his sleeping face. With two children of her own, a boy and a girl, she still had plenty of room in her heart to adore her little nephew. The "ding" of the toaster interrupted her gaze.

"I'll join you in the kitchen in a minute, Em. I'm just finishing up a letter to Ma." Evelyn smoothed the papers before her and read silently.

Dear Ma,

Harold and I hope and pray that you are managing through this Great Depression. Although times are difficult, we are so very fortunate that Harold has employment. At the moment he is working as a route man at a local laundry business. Emily and Henry's business at Klein and Gmahle is doing quite well, all things considered.

Thank you for asking about my dear friend, Doris. She married a businessman and currently resides in nearby Norwalk. We see her occasionally at holiday gatherings and such.

Emily and I were so excited to hear from Tommy. As you must have heard by now, he has gotten engaged to a young woman named Catherine. They met in Toronto. Emily will be taking the train to Canada to visit the newlyweds this summer.

We were also delighted to hear the news of Owen and Sarah Quinn's new baby, another girl to add to their brood! How is Robert doing with the farm? Is Isabella still working in Mrs. Mulherne's dress shop in Fintona? We would also love to hear any news you might have about Annie.

Harold and I joined the First United Methodist Church of Stamford. Emily and I volunteer for various charities at the church, suppers and other events. It is very gratifying to do what we can to help others in these uncertain times.

We are nicely settled into our new house on Hillside Avenue. There's a lot more room here compared to our upstairs/downstairs flat with Emily and Henry. We still have the convenience to shopping and school, not to mention Emily and Henry right next door!

Please send my regards to Sarah and Owen, Isabella, Robert, Annie, and Hannah Curran. You are always in my thoughts and prayers.

With love,
Evelyn

"Toast is ready," Emily called.

"I'll be right there." Evelyn folded the letter and sealed it in its envelope. She brushed it against her cheek, envious of its journey into Ma's hands. An ancient ache for an assurance of Ma's love tugged at her insides. How could a mother let her children go so far away? Evelyn knew she had to let go of these nagging thoughts. Throughout her years in Stamford she had seen her share of people dealing with the pain of illness, loss, grief. Surely, the reliable flow of letters throughout the years had been a manifestation of Ma's love.

Entering the kitchen, Evelyn glanced at the mantle clock and said, "Oh dear, look at the time. It's nearly three o'clock!" Emily's children would need to be met at the schoolyard.

"Yes, but we'll have a moment for our toast and tea. A little peace and quiet for Bobby before his cousins come home and cause a commotion." Emily smiled at the thought of her two lively school age children. "Sit down while the toast is still warm."

"Don't mind if I do." Evelyn sat at the kitchen table, sipped her tea and took a bite of toast.

"By the way, I've set out a bag of groceries in the pantry for you."

"Em . . . you don't have to do that," Evelyn said. She and Harold managed to scrape by on his salary. But Emily would make certain that they did not have to scrimp on food and clothing.

"Don't worry. I've added it to your account." Emily waved her hand, as if waving away the cost of the groceries. Evelyn knew that was exactly what Emily did: as the bookkeeper of Henry's company, she magically made Evelyn and Harold debts disappear.

"And don't forget the clothing for Bobby . . ." Emily pulled up another shopping bag. "Just a few old things young Henry's outgrown." When Evelyn peered inside the bag, she saw brand new clothes fresh from the finest stores, certainly not hand-me-downs.

Evelyn quietly accepted Emily's gifts. "Thank you, Em." She bent across the table and gave her a peck on the cheek. "Why don't you send young Henry over to fiddle around with Harold in the tool shed after work?" Although she and Harold did not have much money, time and attention for Emily's family was plentiful.

"Sure! You know how much Henry adores Uncle Harold." Emily wiped her hands on a dish towel. "Let's bundle up Bobby and take him down to the school yard. Fresh air is good for babies."

"A lovely idea." Evelyn brushed the crumbs from her place-mat into the palm of her hand and shook them into a trash can. "I'll be ready in a minute."

As Evelyn leaned over Bobby's sleeping body, she was overcome with emotion. A hymn she had sung at church came to mind. *This Is My Father's World.* Life was full of mystery and wonder, misery and joy, and Evelyn was determined to relish it all. She no longer relied on gravity to pull her through life. Ever since Mrs. King had died in 1927, she'd felt as if she'd been released from a prison sentence. As Mrs. King had weakened with age, Emily and Henry had finally managed to escape her grip to get married in 1924. Evelyn remembered the day Emily had left Franklin Street. Even Mrs. King had to admit that Emily was getting on in years, and Henry would surely provide well with his business. Reluctantly, Mrs. King had allowed the marriage. Besides, she would still have Evelyn to boss around. Failing in health, she needed Evelyn to tend her every need.

With tears in her eyes, Evelyn had attended Emily's wedding, knowing that her own release was just a matter of time. Mrs. King wouldn't live forever. Evelyn would sneak out to meet Harold after Mrs. King had settled in for the night. They would take a moonlight stroll down North Street, or a ride in his new Flivver. Harold's signal was a pebble tossed against the window pane of her attic bedroom. One time Mrs. King had suspected Evelyn's nocturnal visits.

"Where have you been?! I've been pounding on the wall for you to come and help me, and here you are, out gallivanting with some lowly delivery boy, and I am left suffering. After all I've done for you! Now what would your father have said?" Mrs. King had heaved her chest and fanned her face, overcome with the exertion of chastising Evelyn. The mention of Da had stung, but had made

Evelyn all the more determined to be more careful in slipping away from her jail-keeper. Da would have loved Harold.

Then, one day in 1927, Mrs. King died. Without delay, Harold and Evelyn got married at Saint Andrew's Church with Doris as the witness, Emily, and Henry at the altar beside them. Miss Peartree no longer lived in Stamford, as she had retired and moved in with her niece in Philadelphia. Evelyn was amused by the wedding gift she had sent: a copy of *Bartlett's Familiar Quotations*.

And now, even though the world was in the midst of a great depression, she had never been happier. A cozy house with her husband Harold and baby Bobby, right next door to Emily and Henry Klein and their two children. Life was good!

As she raised Bobby to her shoulder, he stirred and then settled into the crook of her neck. She tiptoed to the backdoor where the stroller was parked. Gently laying him within, she promised him she'd be a loving mother forever. There would be no "good-byes" for this family. She turned her face upwards to the May sun and with closed eyes, she whispered a prayer, thanking Da for giving her this life in America, and thanking God for Emily.

About the Author

Gweneth Howard Mahoney is the granddaughter of Evelyn and Harold Howard. She is the second of three daughters born to Robert Weir Howard and Barbara Davis Howard, so she knows a little something about sisters. She is an adjunct lecturer in Early Childhood Education at Towson University. Gwen has several more children's book manuscripts forthcoming.

About the Illustrator

Betsy Howard Carnes is also the granddaughter (the first) of Evelyn and Harold and is the author's older sister. She has created many illustrations for young people, but few as personal as this family legend. She hopes her own story of coming of age could be told with as much grace through hardship as Evelyn shows.

Three Howard sisters: Betsy, Gwen, and Kathy, 1985

Author's Note

This is a work of fiction, loosely based on memories, photos, historical documents, and family stories. I cannot take credit for knowing the thoughts, words, and details of Winnie and Emily's journey. I took great liberties with characters, names, places, and descriptions, many of which are entirely fictional. For example, I was able to locate the handwritten ship manifest from the California listing passengers, including Emily, Winifred, and Lizzie Askin. There were also records of the sisters being detained until their aunt met them in person. On the other hand, I created fictional boarding-house characters, collapsed different family members into a few, and used fictional names in those cases. Nonetheless, it was my hope to have captured some of the universal truths about family, immigration, separation from loved ones, and most of all, sisterhood.

I am indebted to all the bearers of family lore and Irish history: Norman Weir, Chris Matthys, John Henry Klein, Natalie (Sally) Weir, Therese Kelly, Joan Mahoney, Catherine Mahoney, Marcia Araki Howard, Barbara Howard, and Robert Weir Howard. A special thanks to Norman for driving me around Fintona and Clabby to see the landmarks described in this story. Thank you to my proofreader and only daughter, Jessica Mahoney.

A special thanks to my writing critique group for reading and advising: Nora Frenkiel, Emily Levitt, Shawn Nocher, Sherry Audette Morrow, and Jill Morrow Schapp. Their advice, guidance, and support was invaluable.

It should be noted that I have made use of lyrics to Evelyn's favorite hymn, "This Is My Father's World," Maltbie D. Babcock, 1901, for several subtitles and chapter titles.

On the following pages are actual photos from Eveyln's photo album, and John Henry Klein's family roots expedition in 1971. To see more historical photos related to this story, please visit: www.criticalchristian.org and find the link to *Two Blossoms on a Single Stem.*

Moffat Plantation House. It no longer exists.

Emily and Winnie's first home in Clabby.
Photo taken 1971. The house still exists.

Weir house in Corbally, circa 1971.
The section on the left is the original farmhouse where Emily and Winnie lived.
The larger, two-story addition was added later. This house no longer exists.

Evelyn, young friend (possibly Doris),
and Emily, around 1910.

Emily and Evelyn, around 1910.

Doris and Evelyn, 1921.

Evelyn, 1921, on Franklin Street.

Evelyn and Harold at the beach, 1926.

Harold, Baby Bob, Evelyn, 1932.

Robert Weir Howard, 1933.

Made in the USA
Middletown, DE
08 September 2015